Born and raised just outside Toronto, Ontario, **Amy Ruttan** fled the big city to settle down with the country boy of her dreams. After the birth of her second child Amy was lucky enough to realise her lifelong dream of becoming a romance author. When she's not furiously typing away at her computer she's mum to three wonderful children who use her as a personal taxi and chef.

Also by Amy Ruttan

Perfect Rivals...
Tempting Nashville's Celebrity Doc
Unwrapped by the Duke
Alejandro's Sexy Secret
His Pregnant Royal Bride
Convenient Marriage, Surprise Twins
Navy Doc on Her Christmas List

Sealed by a Valentine's Kiss miniseries

Craving Her Ex-Army Doc
His Shock Valentine's Proposal

Discover more at millsandboon.co.uk.

THE SURGEON KING'S SECRET BABY

AMY RUTTAN

MILLS & BOON

First published in Great Britain 2017
by Mills & Boon, an imprint of HarperCollins*Publishers*
1 London Bridge Street, London, SE1 9GF

Large Print edition 2018

© 2017 Amy Ruttan

ISBN: 978-0-263-07284-6

MIX
Paper from
responsible sources
FSC™ C007454

This book is produced from independently certified FSC™ paper to ensure responsible forest management. For more information visit www.harpercollins.co.uk/green.

Printed and bound in Great Britain
by CPI Group (UK) Ltd, Croydon, CR0 4YY

This book is dedicated to all the mothers waiting next to their child's hospital bed. Waiting for a miracle.

And this book is also dedicated to all those doctors out there who perform those miracles on tiny humans.

Thank you.

PROLOGUE

Isla Hermosa—war-torn country

"I NEED A unit of packed cells—stat!" Reagan shouted over her shoulder. But no sooner had the words left her mouth than another explosion rocked the mobile hospital unit.

She had a wounded man open on her table, and instinctively she threw her body over her patient's to try and prevent dust and debris from entering into the exposed body cavity.

After working in this war-torn place for over a year, throwing herself over a patient came as second nature. It shouldn't have to, but such was the nature of war.

Isla Hermosa had been a beautiful, peaceful country once. A paradise in the Atlantic for vacation-goers. A country founded by Spanish and Greek settlers over seven hundred years ago, full of pristine beaches and tall palm trees.

Now the beach they were on just held the charred remains of its tall palms, and the blue sky was blackened with plumes of smoke rising from the capital. Dust filled the hot air, making it hard to breathe. There was no relief.

It was not ideal to be operating out in the open like this, but it was stiflingly hot on the beach, and being closed up in a tent in this humidity would not make matters any better. What they needed was a hospital, but that was impossible. Most of Isla Hermosa had been taken over by the rebellion, and Canadian peacekeepers, along with those on Isla Hermosa who remained loyal to the dysfunctional Hermosian King Aleksander, had been pushed out of the city and back to the Atlantic Ocean.

The mortar fire stopped and Reagan went back to work on saving this Hermosian soldier's life. As a trauma surgeon for the Canadian Armed Forces she had seen her share of war-torn countries. As soon as she'd had her medical training she'd joined up for active duty. She wanted to serve her country. To prove to herself.

To whom?

She shook that thought away and continued her

work. It wouldn't matter soon. Her agreed-upon tour of duty was ending and she had to return to the attending position that was waiting for her in Toronto.

She didn't know quite what she was going to do with herself back there, besides work. During patients there was down time, card games and a camaraderie. She didn't really have any one in Toronto. The people she served with were like a family. Not like *her* family, though. Not really, because her real family was cold and barely in her life.

The people she served with were her family.

In Toronto she'd be all alone. Again.

Toronto was her home town in the sense that she had been born there, and knew it well. She had a job waiting for her, but it wasn't really home. Her parents weren't there anymore.

Her parents had retired and moved to warmer climes while she'd served. They hadn't even told her that they sold her childhood home until a letter she'd sent them came back marked "Return to Sender."

Only the Canadian Army had ever wanted her, but she had to return to Toronto. She'd served the

time she'd signed up for and her leave of absence from the Toronto hospital was ending.

The friends she'd made here would forget her soon enough. No relationship ever lasted and that was fine. She was used to that. She didn't want to rely on anyone.

Her parents had taught her well. They'd always told her to make a life for herself. Not to rely on them. So she didn't.

I wish I had someone.

She was annoyed that she'd let that little thought sneak in.

Get a grip on yourself, Reagan.

Now was not the time to get maudlin.

"The packed cells you were looking for," a rich, deep voice said, and her body instantly reacted.

Dr. Kainan Laskaris, the foremost trauma surgeon in all of Isla Hermosa, stood beside her. Kainan always unnerved her. He made her feel exposed, vulnerable, as if he knew the pain she was hiding. Knew all her insecurities.

He was the first man in a long time to unnerve her in a *good* way.

"Thanks," she said, barely glancing at him.

When she'd first arrived there she'd tried to keep him at a distance, but it had never worked.

He'd wiggled his way in and, though they didn't really talk much about personal stuff, she enjoyed his company. And he was a damn fine surgeon.

He hung the unit of packed cells, calmly drowning out the chaos of the war that was going on in the background.

His presence made her very aware of how very close the quarters were in this tent, but he helped her focus. He distracted her from all that was going on outside.

"How do you keep such a calm demeanor?" she'd asked, the first time they'd worked together on the wounded during mortar fire.

"I drown it out. I ignore it. I think of it as thunder, or something else, and focus on the person in front of me. I try to picture my patient's life and on my duty to return this patient to those who love him or her. Clear your mind and picture the life you're saving."

It had worked. The tactic had worked and helped her focus.

She was going to miss working with him.

"Do you need help, Dr. Cote?" Kainan asked, but he was already pulling on a pair of surgical gloves.

If he had been any other surgeon she would have

barked orders to him, as she outranked most in her unit, but there was something about Kainan that commanded respect.

She could never turn him down, and she didn't want to. He knew what she needed in surgery without asking. He was like a second set of hands for her.

"Thank you," she said. "Are there no others?"

"No, the fighting is ending. The rebels are being driven back—that's the last report that I heard."

Kainan went straight to work, helping her repair the damage to the soldier.

He shook his head and *tsked* in disgust. "This situation should never have happened."

"I agree," she responded.

She didn't know much about what had caused the once peaceful island kingdom of Isla Hermosa to erupt into revolution, but she knew it had something to do with King Aleksander, after he'd been crowned after his father's death.

The former King, Mateo, had been instrumental in aligning his kingdom with Canada, and had had a good relationship with the country and good trade agreements.

King Mateo had been a great king for more than

fifty years, but his eldest son, Aleksander, was not proving to be so great.

Isla Hermosa had severed its ties with Spain five hundred years ago, so when the revolution had broken out Canada had promised to help. Isla Hermosa had called to Canada and Canada had responded.

Which was why she was there.

"I hope this is over soon," she said as she finished her repair of the spleen. "My orders came in last night and I'm shipping out tomorrow."

"So soon?"

There was a hint of disappointment in Kainan's voice, which made her heart skip a beat.

Don't get hung up. It's probably nothing. You're a good surgeon and he can see that.

The mortar fire had become distant and the unit of soldiers that had been lying in wait to protect the hospital began to move. Tanks were soon going by, kicking up dust.

Reagan cursed under her breath and covered her patient again.

Kainan helped her. She was very aware of his body close to hers as they protected their patient.

"I thought you would stay until the end," he said, after the roar of the tanks had died down.

They went back to work as the dust settled.

"No, a new unit has come in to relieve us. They'll stay until Isla Hermosa is back on its feet."

"That could be some time," Kainan muttered darkly. "I wonder if Isla Hermosa will ever recover from this."

"Hopefully it will. Your country has seen enough bloodshed."

"Yes." There was sadness in his voice.

She wondered if he'd lost loved ones. They worked well together, and he was a brilliant surgeon, but they didn't delve much into personal issues beyond the sphere of this surgical unit.

Which was fine with her.

Even though she knew little about Kainan, there was still camaraderie between them. They'd experienced the war together here, patching up soldiers and civilians. They were friends and she'd miss him.

Even though it would be good to put some distance between them. She didn't want to do something she'd regret.

Live a little.

"I've grown accustomed to working with you," he said, and those dark eyes held her captive.

It thrilled her, unnerved her, this effect he had on her.

Reagan smiled behind her surgical mask. "I like working with you too, but it looks like this is the end."

Kainan nodded. "I guess so."

Reagan finished her repair and began to close up. Her patient would be taken to Spain which was the closest hospital they could get to, where he would be monitored in a military hospital. At least now he would survive the journey.

They didn't say anything as they prepared the soldier for transport, loading him onto the waiting helicopter that would carry him to an American aircraft carrier. A medical plane would take the soldier on to Spain.

When Reagan pulled off her surgical mask and gloves she let out a sigh of exhaustion. She had been working straight for almost twenty-four hours, since the peacekeepers had been pushed back to the beach. It was late afternoon, and though the sun was no longer beating down on them it was still sweltering, and she had the urge to run into the ocean and cool herself off.

Except for the fact that the beach was littered with boats belonging to the allied forces coming ashore.

Kainan was staring back toward the hill where the tall, ancient city gates were. There was smoke rising from the city and he was frowning.

"I'm sorry," she whispered.

She wanted to tell him she knew how he felt, but really she didn't. She didn't know what it was like to lose the country of your birth. To have it mangled and everything destroyed.

She couldn't even imagine what he was going through.

"You okay?" Kainan asked.

Reagan closed her eyes and shook her head. "You don't need to worry about me. I'm just exhausted."

He cocked his head to one side, those dark brown eyes penetrating her to her very core, and she fought back the urge to run her hands through his thick chestnut curls.

"I think there is more. Sadness has come over you."

"I was just thinking of leaving here. I was thinking…" She trailed off, getting choked up.

She didn't want to tell him that she was sad she

was leaving the people she considered friends, the people who were like her family, in order to return to a lonely life in Toronto.

It had never bothered her until now.

"I hate leaving a job undone. There is so much work here, but my tour is over."

He sighed and dragged his hand through his hair. "Yes, there will be many pieces to pick up once the dust settles, but Isla Hermosa will rise again. There have been other wars, other strife that has hit our shores, and we have stood the test of time."

Reagan smiled and they walked in silence back to the tent. There were no more critical patients. Just those with minor wounds that were being made ready for transport off the island.

"Captain Cote, you're officially off duty," said Major Smart as she came to the hospital tent. "You've done a wonderful job, but we're getting ready to pull out. The next rotation is here and you need your rest."

"When does my transport leave, Major?" Reagan asked.

"Zero one hundred. I suggest you get some rest—and that's an order."

Reagan saluted Major Smart and stood there for a few moments. She had been relieved of duty and at one in the morning she'd leave Isla Hermosa and head back to Petawawa, before being formally and honorably discharged from the Canadian Armed Forces.

"You hungry?" Kainan asked. "You look like you need food and rest."

"I do—but don't you have to move to the front with the Hermosian Army?"

Kainan shook his head, a strange expression crossing his face. "Not yet. I have time. Why do you think I came here to help with the wounded when our mobile medical unit is further up the line?"

Reagan smiled. "I've just got used to seeing you hanging around these last few months. Usually getting in my way."

Kainan grinned that mischievous grin which always caused her pulse to race. If they weren't here in the middle of a war... But they were, and Kainan was off-limits. She was leaving in a matter of hours and she wasn't even sure that she'd ever see him again.

"You have a beautiful smile, Reagan."

A blush crept up her cheeks. "What?"

"You never smile for me. You're always so serious."

"This is war. I don't feel much like smiling."

Kainan stopped and took her hand, those intense dark eyes focused on her. She wasn't used to that. She wasn't used to the attention.

"You look tired, Reagan. You need sleep and food."

"I'm fine."

"Come."

It wasn't a request, it was an order, and technically he outranked her. Kainan placed his hand on the small of her back and led her toward the mess tent.

She was so exhausted that she let him get food and a Thermos of coffee, but he didn't let her sit down at a table. Instead he led her outside.

"Where are we going?" Reagan asked tiredly. "The beach is full of armed personnel."

"We're not going to the beach. We're going to my tent. It's in a shady spot and we won't be in any danger."

"There was mortar fire not that long ago," she said, falling into step beside him.

Kainan sighed. "The rebels have surrendered and there's a cease-fire. We should be at peace for a while."

Kainan's tent was on the edge of the Hermosian camp that bordered the Canadian forces' camp. And it *was* in a shady spot, with camouflage netting. They took a seat down in the sand under the awning, and felt the breeze blow in off the Atlantic.

Reagan closed her eyes and let the cool air wash over her.

"Here, drink this." Kainan passed her some coffee.

"I'm supposed to be resting."

She took a drink of the dark, sweet Hermosian coffee. She couldn't remember the last time she'd been able to savor a cup of coffee. Usually she downed it quickly, burning her tongue in the process, as she tried to patch together the wounded soldiers and the unfortunate civilians who'd got in the line of fire.

"If you go to bed now you will be even more tired by the time your transport comes because you won't sleep when you're so stressed. Unwind and relax."

"This is nice," she admitted.

"I will miss you," he said out of the blue, and he smiled sadly at her. "You have been a great friend and you're an amazing surgeon. I've enjoyed working with you."

Reagan was shocked, but pleased, and she squeezed his hand. "Ditto."

"Really?" he asked, surprised.

"Of course."

"You could've fooled me. You're so closed-off around me sometimes."

"Then why will you miss me?"

Kainan grinned. "Because you're brave, compassionate…"

"You just called me closed-off," she teased.

"Compassionate with your patients. You have a kind heart."

She blushed again. "Thank you."

"You're also beautiful."

He ran his thumb across her knuckles. His hands were rough from the dry heat and the tough conditions, but they were strong, surgical hands. And the simple touch was both calming and exciting at the same time.

"You're the most beautiful soldier I have ever seen."

His eyes twinkled and he smiled, causing a dimple to pucker in his cheek under his stubble.

Blood heated her cheeks at the compliment. No one ever paid her compliments. She wasn't sure how to take it.

"Why do you need my approval all the time, Reagan? For goodness' sakes, leave me alone. You don't need validation for something that is so ordinary."

Her mother's harsh words rang in her ears.

She began to tremble, thinking about her mother and the lack of parental compassion she'd had growing up.

"You're trembling." Kainan pulled her close and whispered, "Why?"

"Tired. That's all." She was lying, but she didn't want to think of her mother now.

Kainan held her. She buried her head in his chest, drinking in the scent of him, and the human connection she hadn't realized she'd been craving calmed her.

"Where are you going after we pull out?" she asked, still clinging to him.

"To the front lines," he said tersely. "Tonight."

Her heart skipped a beat. The front lines were dangerous. Even if there was a cease-fire, the capital city of Helicia had become a tangled mess of debris, mines and IEDs. The thought of him getting hurt scared her.

"You're shivering again," he whispered as he rubbed her back.

"I'm just worried about you advancing tonight." She looked up at him. "It'll be dangerous."

He grinned at her. "I will be okay. I will worry about you too, you know."

"I'll be on military transport, headed back to Canada."

"Things happen—and Canada is a long way away. A whole ocean divides us."

He reached out and stroked her cheek, wiping the tears from her face, and before she knew what was happening he was kissing her. Tenderly at first, and then possessively, but it felt so good and she kissed him back, gripping the collar of his tattered linen shirt as if his life and hers depended on it.

"I'm sorry," he whispered breathlessly against her mouth. "I don't know what came over me. I've

gotten so used to being around you, seeing you every day, just the thought of not seeing you…"

She should put an end to it, the kissing, but she just wanted to *feel*. She wanted to give in to the attraction she felt for him. The white-hot lust.

It would be once.

Just one time.

It had been so long since she'd been with someone, since she had any kind of intimacy.

"No apologies—and don't stop." She kissed him again, running her hands through his hair.

"Reagan, we need to stop."

"Why?"

"I'm advancing and you're leaving. What future do we have?"

"Right now, none. But I'm not asking for a future, Kainan. I just want to *feel* tonight. I just want a connection with you. I've been fighting it since I met you."

He nodded, his gaze holding hers. "Me as well."

"So don't stop," she whispered, pulling him into another kiss which seared her very soul.

He stood to his feet, helping her up. "Come."

Reagan thought that he was going to take her

back to her camp, but instead he led her inside his tent, taking her in his arms.

"I want you so much, Reagan. I wanted you the first moment I saw you. But I don't want to make you a promise I may not be able to keep," he whispered against her ear.

"I care for you too. And you don't need to promise me anything. I just want this."

"As you wish," he said, before kissing her again, making her melt into his arms completely.

It was dark outside and she could hear movement. People on the move to the front lines. She rolled over in the narrow cot that she and Kainan were sharing and glanced at her watch. It was midnight. In an hour her transport would be leaving. She had to pack up what little gear she had and get to the rendezvous point.

Kainan was already up and dressed in his uniform, which she'd rarely seen him wear at the mobile hospital. It was a bit surreal, and thinking about him in danger made her stomach knot with unease.

"I was just about to wake you," he said gently.

"Sorry I slept so long here."

"No, it's okay." He leaned over and kissed her. "I have to go with the next transport to the front lines. There is fighting going on in the city. More wounded. I'm needed there."

"I thought there was a cease-fire?" she said, dressing quickly in her wrinkled clothes.

"There was, but some insurgents have been found hiding in the city. It will be taken care of."

He said that with a finality which sent a shiver down her spine.

She finished dressing.

He took her in his arms and held her close.

"Please be safe," she whispered, drinking in the scent of him. She wanted to remember every moment of this time with him, and she sent up a silent prayer that he would be safe.

"You too, Reagan. My beautiful Reagan. I shall never forget you." Kainan kissed her. "Come, we'd better go."

They walked out of his tent and saw the Hermosian camp was a flurry of activity. He walked her as far as he could, to where the Canadian forces were packing up what they could, ready to join the Hermosian Army.

"I'll never forget you," she said, and she wouldn't.

How could she forget him? A man who had seemed to see past her façade. A dangerous and yet gentle man, and one heck of a surgeon.

A man she'd been proud to serve with.

"Ditto."

He kissed her hand one last time and then headed toward a large transporter that was waiting for him. He climbed up into the back of the armored vehicle and waved at her as the truck rumbled away into the darkness toward the front lines.

Please keep him safe.

Reagan headed back to the tent she shared with another surgeon. She packed up her kit bag and then waited for her transport.

It was past 1:00 a.m. when the radio in the mess hall crackled to life.

"Explosion. Hermosian medical transport attacked. All personnel dead."

The words hit her like a rock and her stomach knotted. She closed her eyes and bit her lip as the words hit her.

Maybe it wasn't Kainan's transport?

She wanted to stay and find out if his name was on the list, but her transport came then.

She was airlifted to the waiting Canadian vessel which would take her back home. She was assigned her berth, but as soon as she'd set her bag down she found the nearest commanding officer from her unit.

"General Travis, do you have a list of casualties from that Hermosian medical transport?"

General Travis shook his head. "No, not a full list, but I know who you're asking about and I'm sorry, Captain Cote. I know that you worked with Dr. Laskaris, but his name *is* on the list of those who perished. His dog tags were found and not much else. An IED near the palace went off."

Reagan's stomach twisted and she ran to the side of the boat, losing what little food she'd managed to eat since leaving Kainan and arriving on the transport, over the side of the ship.

General Travis patted her back. "I'm sorry, Captain."

She nodded, and managed to keep the tears at bay.

This was why she kept people at distance, why she never let anyone in. Because in an instant they could be taken from you. They left. They died.

Kainan had wormed his way in past her defenses and now he was gone.

She was alone.

Completely alone.

She should have known better. She was *meant* to be alone.

It was easier that way.

CHAPTER ONE

A year later, Toronto

REAGAN WALKED THROUGH the halls of the hospital in a daze. There wasn't enough coffee in the world to wake her up. It had been a long shift at the hospital and then her infant son had a bad night. The cot in her son's hospital room in the pediatric critical care unit wasn't exactly comfortable, and she could use a break to go home and have a shower.

The problem was there was no one to give her a break.

It was just her and Peter in the world.

A year ago she'd spent an unforgettable night in Kainan's arms. A night that she would cherish forever. Then he'd gone to the front lines and died for his country.

She'd come back to her life in Toronto, empty and alone.

Although it had turned out she was not completely alone, because her one night with Kainan had resulted in pregnancy.

It was the best gift.

A piece of Kainan.

A child.

Someone to love.

And she wasn't going to make Peter feel like a mistake, the way her parents had made *her* feel.

Nothing she'd ever done had pleased them.

Her father had never wanted kids. When her mother had got pregnant with Reagan he'd stuck around, but he had always been distant. Over time, her mother had come to resent her for causing such distance in her marriage.

There had been times when she'd got shreds of love and affection from her mother, but it they had been few and far between.

She'd thought maybe being grandparents would soften her parents' hearts.

She'd been wrong.

When she'd told her mother about the situation—about the baby and the father dying—her mother's response had been heartless. Painful.

"Get rid of the problem, Reagan. You can't raise a baby on your own."

"I'm not getting rid of the baby, Mother."

"Then what do you want from me, Reagan?"

Honestly, she didn't know. Some part of her had hoped her mother would change, but she should have known better.

Reagan had always been a burden to them. And her getting pregnant overseas on a mission was just another disappointment for her parents. They were even more disappointed that she'd kept the baby.

As soon as Reagan had found out she was pregnant she'd vowed that she'd protect Peter. She'd give him the love she had never had, the compassion she had to learn by herself.

No one would hurt Peter. *Ever.*

Her parents had never cared about her. They'd only taken care of her because they were legally obligated to do so.

"I've never run from my mistakes, Reagan. That's why I took care of you. At the time, abortion wasn't an option."

Reagan was a mistake. It hurt to hear it time and time again.

She focused on the lukewarm coffee she was drinking.

A baby had never been in her plan, but she was responsible for her actions. There were plenty of single parents out there, going it alone. And she would do the same. She would *never* let Peter feel as if he was an obligation or a mistake.

But what should have been one of the most joyous days of her life, when Peter was born, had quickly turned into her worst nightmare.

In all her years as an intern and then a resident in hospital, and then her time in the field with the Canadian military, serving as a trauma surgeon during natural disasters and being tossed into the fray of war zones, she'd seen many sick children. Critically ill children. It had always been a deeprooted fear of hers that one day, if she ever had a child, something might happen to that child.

She had never been able to handle the thought of it.

And then it had happened.

She'd had Peter.

"Let me see him!" she'd cried, relieved that the birth was over.

Only none of the doctors had answered her.

Marisa, her OB/GYN, hadn't looked at her. It was in that moment that Reagan had realized the baby wasn't crying. There wasn't a sound coming from him at all.

"What's wrong?" Reagan had asked.

She'd craned her neck as Marisa had turned back to her, watching the pediatrician on call with her baby in his hands, blue-grey and barely moving.

It had only been a couple of hours later when she'd learned that her baby had cardiomyopathy and would be staying in the hospital indefinitely. The only reminder of her and Kainan's time together was placed on the list for UNOS and would be staying there while he waited for a new heart.

The nursery she had so painstakingly started to prepare in her small apartment before his birth was still unused, and she hadn't been able to look at it the few fleeting times she'd managed to get home.

Don't think about it—and don't think about Kainan.

Even a year since his death often Kainan crept into her thoughts because Peter looked like him

so much. And she couldn't help but wonder what it would have been like had Kainan lived.

Reagan had had a couple of relationships before Kainan, but they'd failed because of *her*—because she couldn't trust. At the back of her mind she was terrified she'd disappoint, that she'd never be good enough and her heart would be broken. Again.

It was better this way.

She was better off alone.

"Reagan, you look like you didn't get a wink of sleep!"

Reagan rubbed her tired, sore eyes and saw the Chief of Surgery leaning over the central desk, where he'd been studying a chart.

Michael McNeil had been so understanding. He'd trained her as a resident, and encouraged her into the Canadian Armed Forces to expand her skills, and since she'd announced her pregnancy and Peter's birth he'd been accommodating, knowing she needed to work. Right now he was looking at her with pity. Like most people. She hated pity.

"We need better cots on the NICU floor," she mumbled, stifling a yawn.

"Are you going to be able to work with this new doctor?" he asked.

Reagan nodded. She needed this job. It was more pay, and not so much time spent doing surgical rounds. Right now she couldn't do a lot of surgery. A call about a heart might come in at any time, and she needed to be near Peter.

Peter was all she had.

She really needed sleep, but right now she needed work more. It kept her sane. And she was looking forward to this new job. It was more flexible.

"Yeah, I'm good." She walked to the other side of the central desk and poured herself another cup of coffee into a plastic cup and capped it.

"Good. I know things have been hard—"

She held up her hand to cut the chief off. "Michael, I'm okay. I need the work. I *love* the work. And Peter is not that far away. Besides, I'm the only staff member available who knows American Sign Language."

"And you worked in Isla Hermosa as well," Michael said, setting down his chart.

Reagan's heart skipped a beat—which was silly. "The new specialist is from Isla Hermosa?"

Michael nodded. "The Canadian government is giving him asylum. His work is important. That's all I know. And he's a brilliant teacher. I think he will be an asset to our medical students."

"I wonder if I worked with him?" Reagan said, taking another sip of the bitter coffee. The caffeine was doing its job. There had been many other Hermosian physicians out in the field whom she'd worked alongside, but none had been like Kainan.

No one will ever be like Kainan.

She couldn't think about him now.

"I don't know, but the Canadian government was very adamant that he should be given asylum here, and after chatting with him over email I'm very excited to have him on board."

"I'm looking forward to meeting him," said Reagan. "To become a surgical consultant when you can't speak—that's impressive."

She couldn't recall any nonverbal surgeons out in the field on Isla Hermosa. Of course it had been a war zone. Everything was a bit blurry about her experience. Except…

"Well, he could speak before. He was injured at the front and a badly placed endotracheal tube

damaged his vocal cords. I'm told he can speak a bit—but not much, and not for long periods of time. He will be getting corrective surgery here before the New Year, but for now you'll help him."

"Of course," she agreed. She would be happy to. "Does he know about my son and my need for flexibility?"

"No," Michael said. "I told him you needed a flexible schedule, but I thought it best if you tell him about Peter if you want to."

She breathed a sigh of relief. "Thanks."

It was exhausting, constantly explaining Peter's condition to people. It drained her. The new surgeon didn't need to know about Peter, he just needed to know she needed flexibility—which Michael had taken care of.

Reagan fell into step beside Michael as they walked toward his office, where she would meet this Hermosian doctor and they could get to work.

"So, my job consists of interpreting American Sign Language to the students so he doesn't over-tax his voice?"

Michael nodded. "You can use my office to draw up your plans. The first medical students will be coming at one—after the lunch rotation."

Reagan nodded. "Sounds good, Chief."

Michael smiled, and then said softly, "You know we're all here for you, Reagan. If there's anything more we can do..."

Reagan gave Michael a quick nod. She appreciated it, but she didn't want pity or help. Too many people pitied her, and she was tired of it. She was still a surgeon. She was still Reagan Cote, even if it sometimes didn't feel that way.

"I'm good."

"Are you sure?" Michael asked, and there again was that expression of pity that she loathed, directed toward her.

She couldn't push Michael away like she did so many. He had been her mentor when she was resident. He'd taught her compassion and patient care. Things she hadn't been able to learn from her parents. When she'd started her bedside manner had been atrocious, but Michael had guided her, and he had been the one who welcomed her back with open arms when she'd finished her tour of duty.

"I appreciate it so much, Michael. You know that, but I'm fine. Let me work—it keeps me busy."

Michael gave her a quick kiss on the top of her head and whispered, "He'll pull through."

She nodded, blinking back the tears that always threatened to fall when someone started talking about Peter and his condition. Tears that she had learned to swallow because she had to be strong for Peter.

And for herself.

She had to be tough. There was no time for weeping or sorrow. If she gave in to the grief that she was actually feeling she would collapse and be useless.

This new assignment had come at the perfect time. Even though it would take her off her precious surgical rotation, it would keep her at the hospital.

It would keep her busy and close to Peter.

And that was the most important thing.

"You okay?" Michael asked.

"Perfectly."

Reagan plastered on the fake smile she was used to wearing. The one she'd perfected when she was a small girl, because her father had liked her just a bit better when she'd smiled, and had been

nicer to her mother when Reagan had smiled and behaved.

Michael nodded and then opened the door.

Reagan stepped in, seeing the Hermosian doctor had his back to her. Something tugged at the corner of her mind, but she couldn't sift through the fog—or maybe she was having a hard time seeing. Maybe she was so sleep-deprived that this was just a dream.

She began to tremble.

"Dr. Kainan Laskaris—I would like to introduce you to Dr. Reagan Cote, who will be working with you here at the hospital."

The ghost turned around, those dark, expressive eyes of his hollow and wide with shock. The beautifully chiseled face was marred with scars, and on his throat she could see where they had put the botched endotracheal tube. It was almost as if his throat had been slit, the scar was so bad. The dark brown curls were tamed, and streaked with silver. He'd aged. The war had aged him. But he was still devastatingly handsome.

He opened his mouth, as if to say something, but then snapped it shut. And his lips pressed together firmly, as if he was angry.

Her coffee shook in the cup she was gripping so tightly. Her world was spinning and her tight rein on those emotions she'd become so darn good at locking away had gone slack.

She was losing control.

"Never lose control, Reagan. Don't show your weakness to anyone or they'll take advantage of you."

Her mother's voice was screaming in her head.

"Kainan?" her voice finally squeaked out in disbelief.

"You two know each other?" Michael asked.

She waited for that deep, rich voice to answer, *Si.* That affirmation had always made her go a bit weak in the knees.

But of course it couldn't.

His voice had been taken from him.

Instead he just nodded quickly and looked away. As if he was annoyed she was there.

"We worked together on Isla Hermosa during my last tour of duty," Reagan answered, steadying her hand so Michael wouldn't see her tremble. "And we worked well together."

Michael looked visibly relieved. "I'm glad to

hear it! Well, I'll leave you two to it. I'm sure you have a lot of catching up to do."

Reagan didn't even see Michael leave. She just heard the door shut, her gaze focused on Kainan. The man she'd thought was dead.

He stared back at her, but he didn't smile at her the way he'd used to. There was no twinkle in his eyes. Just darkness. It was cold. It didn't faze her, didn't hurt her. She was used to people looking at her that way. It did sting a little, and it gave her confirmation that Kainan was like all the other men she'd met. Like her father. Cold and distant.

"You're alive." It wasn't so much a question as it was a statement of fact, because she'd thought he'd died.

Clearly, he signed in American Sign Language, barely looking at her.

"They told me you had died."

His expression softened briefly. *I'm sorry. There was a lot of confusion at first. I was reported dead for days...*

"Your medical transport was attacked and they found your dog tags in the rubble."

Again, there was a lot of confusion.

It was obvious that he wasn't going to give any further information about it.

Reagan sat down on one of the chairs at the table in Michael's office. There was a stack of materials there. New orientation information for Kainan. She needed to keep busy and not think about why he never reached out to her.

"Has anyone explained all this stuff to you?" she asked as she quickly scanned the binder full of information. If she kept busy she could ignore the racing of her pulse, her trembling hands, the urge to hug him and cry because he was alive.

He shook his head and took a seat across from her. Then he cleared his throat. "Best…come… from…you."

His voice was broken, harsh and guttural. And color bloomed in his cheeks. It was either embarrassment or anger, and knowing Kainan it was most likely anger.

She knew how much he liked to be in control of every situation. He'd commanded all those around him during surgery, and those working with him had followed him blindly.

When he lost control he got angry, but that

would drive him to work harder to solve the problem and regain control.

He was an amazing surgeon.

And this loss of control…

She could only imagine what he was going through. She liked control in *her* life, but she'd learned a humble lesson when Peter was born. Control was just an illusion.

Reagan had to admit that she was angry too. That he was alive and hadn't let her know. He'd known where she was going. He'd known so much about her. Why hadn't he reached out?

Only she couldn't think about that right now. She'd swallow the anger she had and do her job. Keep moving forward as she had always done. If she stopped for a second everything would fall apart.

"Okay," she said, setting her half-empty coffee cup down and opening up the materials. "We can do this together."

Is there anyone else? he signed.

The words were like a slap. He didn't want her here. She realized his body language was more than just embarrassment or anger over his situ-

ation. He was annoyed that she was here, helping him.

Her spine stiffened.

She should have known his attention to her back then had just been seduction. He didn't want to see her again. He'd just been using her.

You wanted it too.

Well, she wasn't going to let him shove her aside. She had a job to do, and anyway she'd got the best part of him. She had Peter, and she didn't regret that for anything.

"No, there is no one else. I am the only doctor here who can interpret American Sign Language and who's free to support you." Now she was really annoyed with him. She wasn't going to let him ruin this job for her.

Fine, he signed. He crossed his arms and leaned back in the chair. His gaze was fixed on her, but instead of anger or annoyance, like before, there was bit of humor. Some smugness.

She wanted to wipe that off his face. "What?" she snapped.

I forgot how prickly you get. How fast your walls go up.

The twinkle she knew so well returned to his

eyes. It was meant to lighten the mood, but she wasn't in the mood for that.

"I get prickly when people are acting like jerks."

"Sorry." He spoke, his voice now barely a whisper.

Reagan shut the binder and, though she knew she was going to regret it, she had to ask. "Why don't you want to work with me?"

The question caught him off guard. Of course this whole situation had caught him off guard. He'd known that Reagan was Canadian, but hadn't realized that she worked at *this* hospital, in *this* city. Canada was a large country. He'd chosen this hospital simply because Dr. Shaw, his otolaryngologist was here.

He hadn't known that Reagan was here. And he hadn't known that she knew American Sign Language or that she would be working in the education part of the hospital. He'd have thought she would be on the surgical floor, wherever she worked, which was where *he* wanted to be, but couldn't be any longer.

How could a man with no voice convey what he needed to his surgical staff during an emer-

gency situation? He couldn't, so his surgical career was over.

Of course that wasn't the only reason his career was over.

His throat tightened at the thought of why it was over. It always tightened when his stress levels rose, and he was certainly stressed now.

Seeing Reagan again was a shock.

And he'd had to hold himself back, because his first reaction when he'd seen her had been to run to her and take her in his arms and kiss her. But this wasn't the time or place.

Nowhere was the time or place.

Still, seeing her again had brought back so many memories. Even though they'd served during a war—a brutal war which had torn his country apart—working alongside her had been some of the happiest moments of his life.

He loved his country, but being called back to serve had been painful. Since his mother had died Isla Hermosa had reminded him only of loneliness and pain.

Reagan had brought back joy into his life.

One of the hardest things he'd had to do in his life was to leave her behind, knowing that she

was going back home to her country and that he was going to the front lines. That he might never see her again.

It had nearly broken him, but it had been for the best that she'd left when all was said and done. Now circumstances had changed and they could never be together. He'd never trap her the way his mother had been trapped in her marriage to his father.

Still, he wanted Reagan—even though he shouldn't. Their year apart had done nothing to extinguish the flames of passion that he felt for her.

He still wanted her.

That long, silky brown hair that was so neatly tied back. The long, graceful neck that he'd once run his hands over. And those lips he'd kissed and wanted to taste again.

Only he couldn't now. Not because he'd lost his voice, but because he would never, *ever* put her inside the dangerous situation he now found himself in.

He was a displaced king, of a country that was precarious and about to sink into oblivion, and he couldn't bring her into that situation.

There were people who wanted to assassinate him. And he would gladly take a bullet for his country, because *he* felt responsible for Isla Hermosa's downfall.

He hadn't been able to control his late brother. Kainan had tried, but his brother had ruined the country in six months after their father had ruled gracefully for fifty years.

Now Kainan was King of a broken, bleeding country. And instead of being there he was here in Canada. First in Ottawa, to recuperate from all the injuries that he'd sustained when the palace had been attacked, and now here at this hospital in Toronto, working and waiting for surgery that might or might not return his voice to him. Surgery he might not survive due to the damage in his throat.

Still, he needed a voice to rule. As King, he had a duty to his country—a tradition to uphold and a service which had so depressed his mother and made her feel trapped.

His father had been a great king, but cold, and protocol had come first. Kainan had watched his mother take second place to Isla Hermosa.

So, no, he couldn't drag Reagan into that. The

crown would die out with him. And maybe it was better that way.

What's first? he signed.

"Have you got your hospital identification yet?" she asked, leafing through all the papers from Human Resources that Kainan had just skimmed.

No. I haven't got that yet.

"Okay, we'll fill out this paperwork and—"

Kainan touched her arm and got her attention. *Why aren't you practicing surgery?*

"I told you. I'm the only one fluent in American Sign Language here who has room in her schedule to assist you."

So this is a punishment for you?

"What?"

Surgery was your life.

She frowned, and continued to leaf through the binder. "It still is, but I was asked to do this and—" She was interrupted by a knock at the door. "Yes?"

A nurse stuck her head round the door. "I'm sorry to interrupt, Dr. Cote, but it's Peter."

Reagan's expression changed. She frowned, looking worried as she slammed the binder shut. "I'll be right up."

The nurse nodded and shut the door.

"I'm sorry, Kainan. I'll try to be as fast as I can but…it could take a while."

Is it a patient? he asked.

Reagan sighed sadly. Her expression was tired, broken, and Kainan couldn't help but wonder who Peter was. Was Peter her husband?

That brief, fleeting thought of her with another man enraged him. It made him jealous to think of another man loving her.

Not that he deserved to feel *any* sense of jealousy when it came to Reagan. He'd given up those rights when he'd let her go in Isla Hermosa.

"No, it's not a patient." Then she sighed again and looked almost as if she was going to be sick. "Kainan, I'm… He's my son. Peter is my son."

She stood up to leave, her body tense.

Kainan was shocked, and sat back as reality sank in. He hoarsely asked, "Your son?"

And then it dawned on him—because he knew that she hadn't had a child when she was serving alongside him in Isla Hermosa.

A cold tendril of dread unfurled in his belly. He jumped up and stood in front of her, blocking her escape and he cleared his throat. "How. Old?"

"He's three months now. He's your son, Kainan."
Reagan didn't offer any other explanation.

"Never trust women, Kainan. Never. Your mother tried to hide you from me when she wanted to divorce me, but you were a prince of Isla Hermosa. She had no right to do that. But she did try. Women are fickle. They are not devoted, they only think of themselves. Never trust them. Close your heart to them or you'll be hurt!"

Kainan didn't want to hear his late father's voice in his head. He'd been a fine king, but a terrible husband and father.

Still, Reagan hadn't told him he had a son.

"I have to go and check on him. Kainan, please move."

Numb, he stepped to the side so she could open the door.

Of course Kainan was going to let her go, but he needed more answers. His *son*? It couldn't be. Why was his son at the hospital? Why was a nurse taking care of him?

He dashed after Reagan, cursing himself inwardly because he couldn't call out to her to stop,

but he caught up with her quickly and grabbed her arm, holding on to her.

She tried to shrug out of his grip until she saw it was him and relaxed.

My son? he signed.

"Yes."

Why didn't you tell me I had a son? Were you trying to hide him from me? He instantly regretted the words. They were so much like something his father would have said.

Her eyes narrowed. "I thought you were dead. They told me you were dead. I wouldn't hide him from you—you know that."

He wanted to believe that, but his own mother had tried to hide him from his father when she was pregnant.

"I never wanted you locked away in the palace, Kainan. I didn't want you locked away like me. I tried to leave, but I couldn't hide you from him either," his mother had said on her death bed. *"I just wanted us to be happy. To be free. I didn't want you to grow up with him as a father."*

"Why?" He'd felt as if his life was a prison sentence. He was guarded and watched all the time,

and though surrounded by people he'd always felt alone. *"Why did you tell him?"*

"I had to. I loved him." His mother had sighed. *"I am sorry I am leaving you. You will never be free. Even as the spare. You will never be your own man. I wanted more for you, Kainan. I'm sorry."*

His mother had died then, and his father had told him woman weren't to be trusted.

"Never trust a woman, Kainan. Never."

Kainan rubbed his temple, where a pounding headache was brewing.

Reagan didn't hide your son from you. She thought you were dead.

That was little consolation to him at this moment.

"I have to go see him," Reagan whispered.

What is wrong with him? he asked as they waited for the elevator.

"Cardiomyopathy." There was a glitter of moisture in her eyes as she cleared her throat. "He was born that way. He was born with a failing heart."

Oh, God.

His heart sank. It was too much. He'd learned

he was a father and that his son was dying all in the same day.

He was no fool. He knew the severity of cardiomyopathy in a child.

Run. Turn and leave.

But he couldn't do that either. He was not the cold, unfeeling man his father had been.

The elevator dinged as the doors opened, and they stood to the side as people got off, before getting in.

Kainan didn't say anything as they rode in silence. Everything was still sinking in.

He had a son.

And his son was the Crown Prince of Isla Hermosa.

He felt bad for inflicting that burden on him. And his son was ill. Cardiomyopathy in an infant was horrific, and Kainan could only assume that he was on the UNOS wait list for a new heart, because that was his only chance at life.

Reagan led him to the NICU, giving him a disposable gown and mask. He didn't really hear anything that anyone was saying as he was led into the room.

In the far corner stood an incubator that was covered with a blue blanket.

His heart was hammering.

He had never wanted a child. He didn't want to sentence any child to a life where he couldn't live, where he was under constant scrutiny. He'd never wanted a family. Relationships didn't work. His father and late brother had shown him that. He didn't want to trap a woman the way his mother had been trapped.

Reagan raised the blue blanket and Kainan gasped as he saw a baby with dark hair. A baby who looked like him and Reagan.

A baby hooked up to a machine.

His heart ached to hold him. It was instant love. It surprised him.

This child was the future of his country. But how could a voiceless king and a broken-hearted crown prince rule a country that was already broken and bleeding?

His heart shattered and guilt washed over him. Reagan had done this on her own. He hadn't been there. He'd failed her. He'd failed them both.

All Kainan could do was turn and leave.

His heart was breaking along with his son's.

CHAPTER TWO

THERE WAS SUCH a flurry of activity that Reagan forgot Kainan had followed her in. When Peter was stable again, and she'd spoken to the doctors, she turned to introduce Kainan to Peter's team. But Kainan had slipped out.

Where did he go?

That was her first thought, and then she was disappointed that he'd left. He hadn't even come over to the incubator. She'd lifted the blanket and he'd looked once, before she'd turned her attention to the nurse. Then she'd drowned out everything else. Her main focus had been her son.

With every day that she stepped through those doors, rinsing her hands, a deep, dark part of her told her over and over again that any future with her son became darker and darker.

The other part of her—the part that had sustained her since she'd found out she was carrying Kainan's child—told her not to give up hope.

To keep going.

To be strong.

To drown out everything else and pour all that she had into her son.

And that was what she did. Day after day since he was born.

She had no other choice.

So she hadn't noticed when Kainan had left because he'd never been there before. She was used to being on her own.

Reagan turned back to Sophie, Peter's nurse in the PCCU. "I'm only a text away."

Sophie nodded. "Sorry for dragging you away from your work. I know your first priority is to work with the new Hermosian doctor."

"My first priority is Peter. *Always.*"

Reagan smiled and gave Sophie's arm a squeeze. She wanted to tell Sophie that Kainan was Peter's father, but she couldn't really form the words. Like Sophie, everyone in the hospital had been told that Peter's father was dead.

And that was not the case.

Kainan was alive. He'd have rights over Peter. She would no longer be in complete control. Kainan would have a say, and that made her nervous.

Kainan might return to Isla Hermosa. What if he wanted to take Peter with him?

Don't think about it now.

She didn't want to make herself sick with worry.

"You okay, Reagan?" Sophie asked.

"Yes. I'm fine. I'll swing by later, Sophie, if I don't hear from you before then."

"Okay, Reagan."

Sophie turned back to the incubator and Reagan sent a mental kiss to her boy, since at the moment she couldn't actually kiss him. She'd only kissed him once, before he was intubated.

Her heart ached at the thought that maybe she'd never be able to really kiss him, see his eyes open and look at her in wonder.

Focus. Find Kainan.

Once she was out of the PCCU she peeled off the disposable gown and mask, tossing them in the nearest receptacle. She was contemplating how she was going to page Kainan when she saw that he was pacing at the end of a dead-end hall near the PCCU.

All the annoyance and anger she'd briefly had for him walking out on their son melted away. She

put herself in Kainan's shoes. He'd just learned he had a son and that same son was gravely ill.

She remembered how she'd felt when she'd found out that Peter was so ill. When they'd whisked him away from her. When she hadn't heard any wail when he was born and she'd been left alone.

Still, he had left.

"You left?" she said gently.

Kainan's dark eyes were a bit wild, and he ran his hand through his thick, dark curls. He nodded and signed, *Sorry.*

"It was a lot to take in. I'm sorry I didn't prepare you better."

Hard to prepare for that. Hard to prepare for learning about a son you never knew you had. He closed his eyes.

"Are you okay?"

I will be fine. The question is, are you? Are you okay?

The question took her aback, because she *wasn't* fine. How *could* she be fine? Her son was ill, Kainan was alive, and she needed sleep. No, she wasn't fine.

"I'm okay." *Liar.* "I should've told you sooner."

You didn't even know I was alive until earlier today.

"True."

They both smiled then, and a bit of the tension melted away.

What's wrong with him? Kainan signed finally. *You said before, but...*

"Cardiomyopathy." The word stuck in her throat. She rarely said it out loud, because if she said it out loud it became real. And she didn't want it to be real.

She was deluding herself. It was *very* real—and scary.

At least she didn't have to explain what cardiomyopathy was to Kainan. He understood the gravity of the situation.

Is he on the transplant list?

"Yes. We're waiting."

How terrible for you. How do you do it?

A spark of anger flared up in her. It was an innocent enough remark, but it had cut her to the quick.

How do you do it?

How could she *not*? There was really no choice in the matter. Just one foot in front of the other.

"There's no choice," she said wearily.

No. I suppose not. Kainan scrubbed a hand over his face. He didn't sign anything else.

Reagan was waiting for him to sign *I'm sorry I wasn't there for you.* Or *Let me help*, but he didn't offer any of these things.

Instead he signed, *Is he stable now? Can we get back to work?*

It was a slap to the face—but then again a lot of stuff had happened to Kainan in a very short span of time. Still, he hadn't even asked their son's name.

Don't take it personally. It's a lot to process.

She'd been disappointed before. Countless times, when her parents had been too busy for her.

"I need help, Mom. Please. I'm tired and Peter is sick..."

"It was your choice to have the baby, Reagan. I told you to get rid of it."

Her mother's callous words still haunted her.

What's wrong? Kainan signed.

"Nothing."

Your expression says otherwise.

"He's stable," she said, answering Kainan and yet ignoring his questioning.

Good.

There was a hint of relief on his face, but only a brief hint. Reagan hoped it was in regard to their son, but again she'd been disappointed before.

"Let's get back to Michael's office and we'll go through everything," she offered.

Kainan nodded and fell into step beside her. There was silence between them, which was good, because right now she was having a hard time to keeping it all together.

Kainan listened to Reagan go over protocols and some other things that he couldn't seem to focus on. All he could think about was taking care of Reagan and Peter. Doing his duty to them.

Even though it would kill him to trap them both in royal protocol.

If his brother had still been alive there wouldn't be this guilt about forcing Reagan into this life Kainan never wanted. He was the "spare," so he's pursued medicine in order to escape Isla Hermosa. He'd gone to medical school in Switzerland and worked there. He'd been happy.

He hadn't ever planned on returning to Isla Her-

mosa after his brother became King, but then war had broke out and his brother had been killed.

Kainan's freedom had evaporated then. It had been obliterated.

Inside he was screaming and raging, but if he tried to let it all out there would be no sound, and that made him rage all the more at his own stupidity. Yet he still wanted Reagan, and now his son. She'd been alone. She shouldn't have been alone.

I should never have let Reagan go.

If he'd have been with her... He didn't finish that thought, because it wouldn't have changed the outcome at all.

Their son would have been born with cardiomyopathy anyway. That was if he'd survived being born in a war-torn country. The thought made his stomach clench. He tried not to think about it.

"Alek, you have to surrender. It's done. Too many lives have been lost!"

"I will not surrender! Father never would've backed down."

"He would if innocent blood was being spilled. What you're doing is folly!"

"You just want the crown for yourself, Kainan. I know you."

"You don't know me. You're completely absurd. I never wanted this. Never."

"Then why are you here?"

"To save your life. You're my brother, Alek..."

"I'm your half brother."

"Half, then—but still I'm here to save you."

"Why?"

"Because Father loved you. I'm doing this for Father."

Alek had sneered and shaken his head.

"Always trying to please Father. But he's dead and I am King. I will always be King."

Kainan shook those thoughts away. They were treading on dangerous ground. They were threatening his control. He'd tried to save his half brother's life before Alek had been overthrown. He'd been trying to drag Alek out of the palace to safety just before the IED had gone off in the throne room.

Kainan had survived the blast, but had lost his voice for his brother...his King.

In the end his brother hadn't survived after the explosion. So it had all been for naught.

Which now made *him* King and his critically ill son his heir.

His son who was dying.

"Kainan, are you okay?"

He turned and saw Reagan was looking up from the piles of paperwork.

"Overwhelmed?" she asked gently.

He smiled. "Under…" Only he couldn't finish the word because his throat closed up, He felt humiliated by it.

Her expression softened. "Statement? Understatement?"

Then she smiled. That warm and friendly open smile which had won him over. She'd always tried to act so strong, but when he'd seen her smile at wounded soldiers, offering them compassion, he'd been won over time and time again. Reagan had reminded him of his mother—not in looks, but in strength and fortitude.

His mother Ariana had been compassionate, strong, independent. She'd loved his father, even though his father hadn't seemed able to love her back in the same way.

When his mother had died he'd been so lonely. There had been no love in the palace. His father had stood on formality. As had his elder half

brother Alek. Only his mother had given him affection.

Reagan hadn't known he was a prince. She'd been so honest. So warm. He'd craved that warmth. Needed it like air. She'd treated him like everyone else on the unit and with her he'd been himself. There had been no formality. No protocol. It had been nice to be himself for a change, instead of Prince Kainan.

If there hadn't been a war... If he was still the spare...

He didn't want to drag her into the tumultuous situation that was still happening in his country. Still, she'd borne his child and she would be in danger if word got out. If he married her he could protect her. He had to do right by her, even though that would mean her life wouldn't be her own anymore. Even though he would be condemning her.

Yes. That. He rubbed his temples, felt his throat tightening again.

"I'm sorry there's so much. I swear we're almost done with the orientation."

Can we take a break? he signed.

She cocked an eyebrow. "A break?"

Coffee?

He had to get out of this room. He felt as if he was suffocating again. Like when he'd woken up after the blast and not been able to breathe, with a tube in his throat, burns on his body.

"Okay..."

She seemed unsure. Confused.

He was confused too—about this whole situation.

When he'd felt this way in the past, surgery and practicing medicine—his work—had helped him get through so much. Saving lives made sense to him. It made sense of this mixed-up world.

And he couldn't do that anymore. He couldn't be a proper surgeon because he couldn't speak, and couldn't sign when his hands were busy. He couldn't lead his broken country for the same reason. He was trapped in limbo.

They walked in silence to the coffee cart.

Even though there were Hermosian guards all through this hospital, and he was being monitored by the Canadian government, no one besides those watching him for his own protection knew he was King.

He was free here.

Kainan could breathe—although he hated hid-

ing here until the surgery was done. He wanted to be on the front lines, saving lives.

Even though he didn't have a voice.

He would soon enough.

That was if it was successful. Sometimes Kainan was positive that he wasn't going to survive the surgery.

Reagan ordered him a coffee, just as he liked it. Hot, dark and rich. No sweetener. She was so thoughtful and he was a monster.

You remembered, he signed.

"You drank it every day religiously, Kainan." She wrinkled her nose. "I can't stand black coffee. I don't know how you do that."

Kainan took a sip. It didn't taste as good as the Hermosian coffee he was used to, but it would do.

Hermosian coffee is much better. It is naturally sweet.

Reagan snorted. "I remember what it tasted like. Black coffee is black coffee."

No, it is not. This is nothing compared to what my country grows.

"That we can agree on. Hermosian coffee *is* better," Reagan said as she dumped sugar in hers.

He shuddered and she made a face at him, making him smile.

They wandered over to a table in the hospital atrium. Snow was falling gently. He was still not used to snow, but it had a nice calming effect.

"What do you think of snow?" she asked.

Cold. He took a sip of his coffee.

"Yes. It must be a culture shock for you."

A bit. He nervously began to flick at the plastic spout on his coffee cup. *Our son...*

"Peter," Reagan whispered softly, a bloom of pink on her high round cheeks.

An interesting name.

"I always liked it—and Peter Pan was the boy who never grew up." Her voice trembled, but only for a moment. "It suits him."

Peter Pan lived forever by not growing up, yes?

"Well, I suppose so. He never aged as long as he stayed in Neverland."

There you go.

Peter. His son was named Peter. Though Kainan hadn't put Peter Pan and his son's name together at first. When she'd said his name was Peter all he'd been able to think of was St. Peter, the patron saint of fisherman.

Isla Hermosa had a thriving fishing industry, so the thought of St. Peter made him happy, but it frightened him all the same. Peter was a prince.

"You're frowning again," Reagan said.

He smiled. *I frown a lot lately.*

"Why?"

I've been through a lot. Then he sighed. *I suppose we both have.*

"Our time in Isla Hermosa feels like a lifetime ago." Pink tinged her cheeks again. "I am glad you're alive. I didn't tell you that."

Kainan's heart melted. *I'm glad to see you again too.*

"So, Michael told me you're awaiting surgery for your voice?"

He clenched his coffee cup. *Yes. I hope it works.*

Kainan didn't tell her the risks he was taking. The chances that he wouldn't live through it. She didn't need to know.

Reagan nodded. "I'm sure it will, although I'm sure scar tissue is an issue in your case?"

Kainan's stomach turned. It was indeed adhesions and scar tissue that were impeding his throat. Choking him from the inside out.

I don't want to discuss it.

"Fair enough," she said.

He felt bad, but he didn't want to think about the surgery. He needed his voice by the New Year, because on January first he was supposed to be on a plane to Isla Hermosa to attend his own coronation.

Without his voice he was trapped. He was blessed that he knew American Sign Language, but without his voice he couldn't properly rule and nor could he practice medicine. And without the surgery he might die.

So he was trapped. There was no choice over his surgery. It had to be done.

A ring tone sounded and Reagan glanced down at the phone in her hand, frowning.

Peter? Kainan signed, his heart sinking.

"No, incoming trauma. I'm needed," she said. "It must be a lot of trauma coming here or I wouldn't have been called in to help."

Go, Kainan signed. *I can find my way around.*

"Not everyone knows ASL."

Kainan pulled out his phone and typed in the word *Go*. His phone repeated it back. She smiled at him.

"I'll be back as soon as I can."

He nodded and watched Reagan disappear, a pang of jealousy coursing through him. How he wished he could be in the fray with her. Like old times.

He tossed the coffee cup in the garbage and wandered through the hospital.

He wanted to be free. And even though he wasn't in a palace, he was alone and shackled here.

You're not alone. You have Reagan.

Only he didn't have Reagan. She wasn't his. Not yet.

His stomach turned with guilt at the life he was going to impose on her.

And he hated himself for it.

CHAPTER THREE

THE INCOMING TRAUMA took longer than Reagan had expected. A multi-vehicle crash with multiple traumatic injuries kept her in surgery for hours, and by the time she got out it was evening. She was exhausted, and wondering what had happened to Kainan.

He wasn't answering his pager at all, and she couldn't help but wonder if he had gone home.

She couldn't really think about it right now. She hadn't heard from Sophie, Peter's nurse, since she'd gone to see Peter earlier. Which was good. Of course it was protocol not to disturb a surgeon when operating. Still, no one had come to find her afterward. So Peter had to be okay.

It had been the longest stretch in a while since she'd got an update and she was worried.

She'd worry about Kainan later. Right now she had to see Peter and make sure that he was all right.

As Reagan approached the pediatric critical care unit she met Sophie coming off her shift.

"Sorry, Sophie. I was in surgery. If you paged me and I didn't answer…"

"It's okay, Reagan. Nothing to mention. Peter is stable, but there *is* something you didn't tell me."

"Oh?"

"You didn't tell me that Peter's father is Dr. Laskaris."

Reagan's eyes widened. "I… What? How did you find that out?"

"He's in there now. At first I wasn't going to let him in to see Peter, per your restrictions, but he said he was his father."

"And you believed him?" Reagan's voice rose an octave.

Sophie blushed. "He offered to take a genetic test. It's still in process. We let him in the unit, but he's not in Peter's pod and he's not allowed to touch him. He's just sitting there, in the room you sleep in, watching him."

Reagan felt terrible for snapping at Sophie.

"I'm sorry, Sophie. You did absolutely the right thing. Dr. Laskaris *is* Peter's father."

"Well, I really grilled him. But you told me Pe-

ter's father died on Isla Hermosa and Dr. Laskaris is Hermosian. Also, you brought him in here earlier, even though he doesn't have privileges yet."

Reagan smiled. "I meant to tell you earlier, but I was in complete and utter shock. I thought he was dead."

Sophie grinned. "I'm sure you were. I know I would be too, in your situation."

Reagan laughed nervously. "You can let Dr. Laskaris in to see Peter whenever he wants."

"I'll make a note on his chart tomorrow."

"Thanks, Sophie. Have a great night."

Sophie waved goodbye as she walked away. And for one moment Reagan envied her because she had freedom.

When Reagan had found out she was pregnant she'd known her life would change, but she'd been expecting diapers, daycare and a messy apartment.

Not this.

Never this.

She buzzed in to the pediatric critical care unit after putting on the gown and gloves that were mandatory. The new shift on the unit had started, and she greeted the people she knew all too well.

Kainan was standing in the little room next to Peter's, watching their son intently through the glass partition. Reagan couldn't read his expression but it didn't matter right now. All that mattered was that Kainan was there.

He was with Peter.

Her father had never been there for her. He'd barely acknowledged her. So to see Kainan with Peter softened her heart.

Maybe he did care about Peter. Maybe she had it all wrong.

"I'm sorry I'm so late," she said, coming up beside him. "I tried paging you, but you didn't answer."

My phone died, he signed. He held it up. *Forgot the charger. It's back at my place.*

"Oh." She cleared her throat. "I'm glad you're here."

He nodded and smiled at her, those dark eyes twinkling.

Me too.

Her heart skipped a beat. "I told Sophie you're his father. A genetic test isn't needed."

It's okay. Actually, I don't mind. I would like it done all the same.

Heat bloomed in her cheeks. "Of course. You need verification. Facts. You are a doctor."

What are you talking about? He looked confused.

"You'll need scientific proof that he's your son."

He frowned. Looked concerned. *No, not at all.*

"Really?" she asked in disbelief.

Really. He turned and looked back at Peter. *In him I see me.*

Her heart skipped another beat, because she'd had that thought so many times when she'd looked at Peter.

She saw Kainan.

"Then why did you agree to the test? Why do you want it?"

Blood types. I'm curious about whether he's a universal donor, like me. It runs in my family.

"He does have a universal blood type."

Kainan smiled. *Good.*

"The cardiomyopathy is genetic, but it doesn't run on my side."

I don't have it either.

"You're sure?"

The royal family of Isla Hermosa has been recorded for a long time, he signed. Then he tensed.

"Uh…what does the royal family of Isla Hermosa have to do with anything?" she asked, confused.

Nothing. I was thinking of something else.

"Okay." Reagan couldn't help but wonder why he was getting so defensive about this. "Still, it's not on my side."

It's not on mine either, he signed. *Stop implying it's my fault.*

"I'm not."

Fine. Good, Kainan signed sharply.

Something was bothering him. "Sorry."

No, I am sorry. Family is a touchy subject for me. The war was hard for so many.

"Yes," she said sadly. "I remember that."

Peter is all I have left.

That made her pause. It made her nervous, thinking he'd take Peter away.

Kainan had rights, but she couldn't lose Peter.

Tears were threatening to escape, and she didn't want to cry in front of Kainan or in front of Peter—even though Peter wouldn't even know it if she did.

In the pediatric critical care unit she had to be strong. She was a warrior. A fighter for her son.

There couldn't be an inch of give. And she didn't want to appear weak in front of Kainan or anyone.

If she did her weakness might be used against her.

Great. Now I'm being paranoid and sounding like my mother.

She had to get a grip. She was stressed, tired and stressed—in that order.

Kainan stepped closer, and before she could stop him he drew her into his arms. Her body reacted instantly to his touch. She closed her eyes, drinking in his scent, her body trembling because she'd never thought she'd experience this again.

She'd thought he was dead.

He was supposed to be dead.

And it had been so long since someone had held her. Her parents never openly showed affection and neither did she. Being in Kainan's arms brought her carefully constructed walls down a little. It was overwhelming to be held by him. Actually to be comforted. Just like it had been the night Peter had been conceived.

"Come," he said, his voice rasping, and she knew that it was a strain for him to speak. But with her head buried in his neck as she drank in

the sensation of being held she couldn't see him when he signed anyway.

Reagan let Kainan lead her out of the pediatric critical care unit.

She was in a daze.

She was exhausted.

Kainan took the gown off her and disposed of it. Then he removed the gown he was wearing.

Reagan shook herself out of the daze she was in. "Peter. I can't leave him."

You can leave him for one night.

"He has no one else."

There's a team of medical professionals in there to take care of him, Reagan. You need sleep and a decent meal.

"I have to stay here," she said firmly.

Reagan, he's stable. If he's not they will page one of us. Come back to my place and I'll get my charger. There you can shower and have a meal. Let's get your things from your locker.

A hot shower and food that wasn't from the cafeteria sounded heavenly, but she was terrified of leaving the hospital.

The nurses and doctors on the pediatric criti-

cal care unit had tried to get her to take a night off every once in a while, but she couldn't do it.

"I can't," she whispered.

My place is right next door.

She cocked an eyebrow. "You're staying at the Royal York?"

He nodded. *Yes.*

"That's pricey."

He shrugged. *I have money, and none of that matters right now. Come, let me take care of you. You shall sleep and I will be on call for Peter tonight. Let me take some of the burden off your shoulders.*

"I would like that…" She cleared her throat as emotion threatened to overtake her, but she controlled it.

Those dark eyes softened as he stepped forward and cupped her face briefly, and the simple touch eased her.

No feeling guilty. To take care of Peter you have to take care of yourself. Let's go.

She nodded and he put his hand on the small of her back, as he'd done when they had gone to his tent in Isla Hermosa. It was nice.

After they'd gathered the small suitcase that she

always kept at the hospital and put on their winter coats—because it was December, and the wind chill off the lake was brutal—they walked out of the hospital together and dashed across York Street. It was quiet, as there were no commuters out and about. However, there were a few hockey fans coming and going.

Kainan raised an eyebrow in question at the hockey-goers, with their blue-painted faces and shouting.

"Leafs. It's hockey."

He nodded, but didn't sign anything, just squeezed her hand as they scurried up Front Street to the entrance of the Royal York hotel.

Through the revolving door Reagan stepped— into another world. She had only been in the Royal York once, and knew it was opulent with its art deco interiors from a golden age of Toronto.

"This way," he whispered, and pulled out a gold card, which meant that Kainan had a suite.

He took her to the private elevator that was used by the elite guests at the Royal York.

He swiped his card and the elevator doors opened. They got on and took the elevator to the top floor. Then he led her down a hallway to the

very end, and swiped the card to open the door to a luxurious suite.

She dropped her bag and stared at the main room with its plush furnishings, and then wandered in to see a king-size bed in another room, a kitchenette. As she approached the window she could see that there was a view of the waterfront over Union Station.

"Wow…" she whispered. "I've never been in one of these rooms before."

He smiled and jammed his hands in his pockets. *Food first, shower or nap?*

"Shower first, if I can. Then food and maybe a nap. But I'm not entirely sure that I'm going to stay here, Kainan. I might have to sneak out and head back to the hospital."

He chuckled and then plugged his phone into the charger on the desk. *You go have a shower and I will order you some food.*

"You don't know what I like," she teased.

I think I remember bits and pieces. Go shower, and then after you eat we'll discuss whether you or I should go back.

"Deal."

She found the bathroom and flicked on the light.

There was a plush white robe and thick, soft towels. Much better than the staff change room. She pulled out her toiletries bag, digging for soap and shampoo.

It didn't take her long to find everything she needed and soon she was turning on the shower. It was nice to have this moment to herself. And she didn't feel rushed here, like she did in the hospital staff room.

This was one of the first times she'd been out of the hospital in months. Paying her rent and utilities was done with a simple app on her phone or over the internet. She had no pets. No plants. Her life was in the hospital.

As she stepped under the shower and let the water wash away her stress she realized that in the hospital she carried the weight of the world on her shoulders. She carried the weight of her son and the life that he might not get a chance to experience. It was only in the safety of the rushing water washing over her that she let it go for the first time in a long while.

She turned off the shower and grabbed a towel to dry her hair and face.

There was a knock on the door. She wrapped

herself in a robe and opened the door. Kainan was standing there.

Are you okay?

"I'm fine."

He pursed his lips together. *You were in there a long time. I was worried you'd fallen asleep in there.*

Warmth flooded in her cheeks. "How long have I been in here?"

An hour. He grinned.

"An hour?" She looked down at her hands, which were wrinkled like prunes from so much water. She must have zoned out.

Come, there's food. You can stay in the robe.

She nodded and followed him out of the en-suite bathroom into the living room area, where there were salads, cheese, fruit and a big bowl of pasta. Her favorite kind too. Fettuccine Alfredo.

He'd remembered.

"Don't think me ungrateful, but how did you order all this?"

Through the computer. The hotel and I have an understanding.

"It smells delicious. I can't remember the last time I had real food instead of cafeteria food."

Then let's eat, instead of standing around here and talking about it.

He motioned for her to sit on the couch and remained standing until she sat.

Always the gentleman.

Even in a war zone. It had always been ladies first. And once, when a particularly crass soldier had got a little handsy with a nurse, Kainan had been there to jump into the fray and put that soldier in his place.

Of course since it hadn't been a Hermosian soldier there had been some international logistics to work out, and eventually both commanding officers had had Kainan and the other soldier duke it out in a boxing ring in the middle of the mobile army hospital.

You're smiling, Kainan signed. *What are you smiling about?*

"I was thinking about that time you boxed that soldier. Totally laid him flat on his back even though he was twice your size."

He made a funny face. *He wasn't twice my size.*

"The man was trained in special ops and he was broad."

Broad is one thing, but "broad" is often con-fused with muscle and mental agility.

Kainan winked and Reagan chuckled.

What made you think of that? he signed.

"I was just thinking about how you're very much a gentleman."

He raised an eyebrow. *Boxing made you think of me as a gentleman?*

"Isn't boxing the sport of kings?"

No, that's horse racing. There was a twinkle in his eyes. *I believe that boxing is the sport of manly self-defense. I believe many fine gentlemen were pugilists a long time ago.*

"Ah, see—there you go. It *is* a gentlemanly sort of sport."

Not anymore. Women box.

"Right, but still..."

Fine, I concede. So, you were thinking of me boxing and you came to the conclusion I was a gentleman?

"No, I was thinking about how you stood until I sat down, and that led me to remember your boxing."

A smile quirked his finely shaped mouth, mak-

ing her recall for a brief moment the way he kissed.

Now you are blushing.

Reagan saw him sign it, but she remembered the sound of his voice and the way he would softly exhale on her neck. It had been a long time since she'd desired anyone, because the last person she'd felt that rush for was Kainan. Since Peter had been born she hadn't had any feelings like that. She had been just numb and existing.

She felt guilty for allowing those feelings to creep back in. So she picked up the bowl of pasta. "I'm glad you remembered my favorite."

Kainan sat back. The spell that had been woven over them was broken and that was a good thing. Reagan didn't have time to start anything up, even if Kainan *was* the father of her baby. Her life revolved around her son and making sure that he survived long enough to have experiences like this.

She had to protect Peter from hurt because there was always an expiration date. Kainan would go back to Isla Hermosa. Kainan would probably leave them again. Her heart could take it—Peter's couldn't.

* * *

The conversation had taken an interesting turn before they'd started eating, and Kainan was trying to remain a gentleman but it was so hard when it came to Reagan. He'd forgotten how much he liked being with her. She brought out a side in him he'd thought he'd buried long ago.

He'd forgotten about laying that officer out in the boxing ring after he'd laid into him publicly outside of the ring when he'd started bothering that Canadian nurse.

Men like that annoyed him.

You could still be a strong, alpha male and respect women.

If only his brother had learned that.

Or his father.

"Mama, why are you crying?"

His mother had wiped away her tears with the back of her hand and then wrapped him up in her arms, holding him.

"Are you sad, Mama?"

"Never, Kainan. Never when you're here."

Kainan had glanced over her shoulder to his mother's bed and seen a newspaper. There had

been a picture of his father, with his arm around a woman who was not his mother.

His father had been a beloved king, but his affairs had been notorious.

Kainan had vowed he'd never be like that. Even if he became King he would never be like that. Of course he'd never thought that he *would* be King. That was something he'd never wanted.

Never.

All he'd wanted to be was a surgeon.

Being King would be a huge responsibility. His life would not be his own anymore. His life would belong to his kingdom and the world. There would be no more privacy. It would be a life of sacrifice and stress.

Could he really do that to Reagan? To Peter?

There was no choice. He had to do what was right and make Peter legitimate.

He glanced up after they'd finished eating and saw that Reagan had fallen asleep. She was curled up on the couch, her head resting on the over-stuffed armrest.

She looked so peaceful.

He hated dragging her into this, but it was the perfect solution. He would marry her and they

would be a family. Then they would return to Isla Hermosa, and maybe he would be able to heal what was broken in his country.

There was a knock at the door. He got up and peeked through the peephole to see his head of security, Andreas, in the hallway.

Kainan opened it.

"I'm sorry for intruding, Your Majesty."

Kainan held his fingers to his lips to silence his security guard and motioned behind him.

Andreas peeked over his shoulder and nodded. "I'm sorry…"

"What's wrong?" Kainan asked hoarsely, rubbing his throat.

"Word has gotten out that the missing Hermosian King is hiding somewhere in Toronto."

Blast. "How?"

"The papers here are running it. Though your picture is not in the papers. Just the story. Someone has leaked it."

Kainan's stomach clenched, and all he could see was his father's face instead of his as he thought of that newspaper on his mother's bed, stained with tears.

Dammit.

Kainan wished that he could let out a few more strings of expletives, but that would wake Reagan, so perhaps it was best that he currently didn't have the ability to do that.

Please keep me informed, Andreas, he signed. *Let me know if the press come anywhere near the hotel or the hospital.*

"We've been keeping a low profile, Your Majesty. The only people on this floor are your security detail and you. Much to our chagrin, we're letting you go to the hospital alone and trying not to be too obvious."

Kainan smiled briefly. *I know that it's hard for you, but it's for the best.*

"What's for the best is for you to remain hidden and safe until you can return to Isla Hermosa."

I am safe.

"Your son is unprotected at the hospital," Andreas said.

A cold rush of dread crept down Kainan's spine. *How do you know about him?*

"I *am* head of security, Your Majesty."

We're done talking about this, Andreas. Keep me posted about the leak.

Andreas pursed his lips together and bowed. "Yes, Your Majesty."

Kainan shut the door and scrubbed a hand over his face. The idea that news about him was getting too close for comfort made him think of his helpless son, clinging to life in a hospital bed. He didn't want the press to find out about Peter. He had to protect him.

Kainan flung open the door and ran after Andreas.

Andreas turned around, confused. "Your Majesty?"

Don't be obvious about it, but protect my son, he signed. *I don't want people coming to the hospital. He needs to protected at all costs.*

Andreas smiled. "Of course, Your Majesty."

Work your magic with administration, but please just keep Peter safe.

"I will, Your Majesty. Right away."

Kainan nodded and turned back to his room. He shut the door gently, so as not to wake Reagan. She was still sound asleep, curled up on the couch.

He approached her and gently scooped her into his arms. She didn't even wake, and he couldn't blame her for being so exhausted. He felt guilty

for not being there when Peter was born. For not knowing and being able to help her.

Kainan carried her to bed and set her down, covering her up. She sighed, but didn't wake. So he stood over her, staring at her face and fighting the urge to touch her, to run his fingers over that graceful neck and through her soft, dark silken hair.

To cup her face and kiss her.

Yet, as much as he cared for her, in this moment his duty was clear.

He cared for her and Peter too much, and in caring for them he would have to burden Reagan. Even as vulnerable as she was, there was no choice.

He needed to make Reagan his Queen.

CHAPTER FOUR

COMFORTABLE. THAT WAS her first thought. But she shouldn't be this comfortable.

Reagan woke with a start and couldn't figure out where she was at first. She was definitely not sleeping on the cot in the pediatric critical care unit, because it was too quiet in here and the bed was too soft.

She sat up and then remembered that she was in Kainan's hotel room at the Royal York.

She heard a sigh and looked over to see that Kainan was sleeping next to her, still in his street clothes. He wore a dress shirt, but the tie that he'd been wearing was gone, and the shirt was unbuttoned. He was lying on top of the covers, his ankles crossed and his hands across his chest.

He looked so peaceful. She wondered how long she'd been sleeping, and when she glanced at the clock on the bedside she saw that it was nine in the morning.

Oh, my God. Peter!

She'd slept through the night. Away from Peter and the pediatric critical care unit.

How could she have been so foolish? What if something had happened to him?

She got out of bed quietly, so as not to wake Kainan. She found her things and quickly dressed, brushing her hair, which had dried naturally and now had a horrible kink in it. That was solved by tying it up in a bun.

She cursed under her breath. Angry at herself for leaving Peter's side. She had been weak when Kainan had convinced her to leave the hospital. She had to be stronger. She couldn't let Kainan sway her so easily.

Who are you kidding?

Even after all this time Kainan was the only one who got through her barriers, and she was angry at herself for letting him through.

Once she was dressed she snuck out of the hotel room, quietly shutting the door behind her. When she turned around, though, she jumped back in surprise to see several men in dark clothes loitering about the hallway.

They'd been talking, but stopped when she shut

the door. They watched her with a sense of reverence, almost awe. Whatever it was, it was supercreepy.

"I'm sorry, miss," one man said, stepping forward.

He had a slight accent similar to Kainan's, and she wondered if they were Hermosian refugees as well.

"Did we wake you? These walls are very thin."

"No, it's okay."

"We're sorry if we startled you. Congregating in the hall before we all head to a…a workshop is not proper."

"It's okay," she repeated.

The man nodded and the other men smiled, stepping back as she scurried down the hallway toward the elevator. She pressed the button and the elevator appeared instantly.

If she didn't know better then she would almost swear those men were security guards.

That's ridiculous. Who are they guarding?

She shook that thought away as she pulled on her winter jacket in the elevator. She pushed through the crowds of people in the lobby of the hotel and

then went downstairs to the concourse level and took the Avenue from the hotel to the hospital.

That way she wouldn't have to go out in the cold.

Reagan weaved her way in and out of the morning rush of commuters who were walking the concourse in underground Toronto from Union Station to all the tall office buildings that connected to the PATH system. When the trains came in the concourse level was flooded with people.

It was a great system, but so crowded during certain times of the day. Like now. But Reagan was a pro at fighting her way through crowds.

At the hospital level, she punched in her access code and took the elevator up to where the staff change room was located. She stashed her coat and the bag of clothes and changed into a fresh pair of scrubs and a lab jacket.

First she would check on Peter, and then she would do her rounds.

You're not doing rounds anymore, remember? You're supposed to be working with Kainan and you left him in the hotel.

Reagan groaned inwardly.

Well, she'd just stay with Peter until Kainan

came to start his shift at ten. That was when they would head down and work with the medical students who were coming in.

When she got to the pediatric critical care unit the morning shift had started and Sophie was back at the PCCU's desk.

"I'm so sorry, Sophie—" Reagan started.

Sophie looked confused. "For what?"

"I fell asleep...at my apartment."

It was a lie, but she didn't want to divulge the fact that she'd spent the night with Kainan, even though Sophie knew that Kainan was Peter's father.

"I went there to take care of some business and just crashed."

"Don't worry about it, Reagan. Nothing happened. Peter's stable." Sophie opened up his file on the computer. "I don't see any notes that you were paged."

"I wasn't paged." Reagan bit her lip and sighed. "Actually, I didn't even check to see if I *was* paged. I just woke up and raced over here. I was feeling incredibly guilty for not being here."

Sophie smiled and gave her shoulder a sympathetic squeeze. "You have the right to sleep. We

all know you're always here and always reachable. Hovering won't heal him."

She knew that, but she didn't want Peter to be alone. Like she had been when she was seven and had had her tonsils out. She'd been alone. Her parents had never come to visit her.

They'd been working.

She'd got a lot of pity then from the nurses.

Even though Peter was too young even to know she was there, she didn't want him to be alone as she had been.

"I have to be here," Reagan said firmly.

It was her duty to be here for Peter. Her parents might be standoffish, but Reagan had sworn she'd never be like that. She *had* to be there, even if she could use a break, but thoughts still ate away at her. Made her feel like a terrible mother.

"I know. I've been a pediatric nurse for a while now, and I know that you need to be here. Peter knows that you're here, but you need to take care of yourself too. When he gets his new heart and gets out of here you're going to have to contend with a baby, and then a toddler. He's not going to know that he has to take it easy, and you'll need your strength for that phase. Usually my sickest

little ones are the ones who are the most mischievous when they get out of here."

Reagan laughed and tried to picture it, though it was hard to see because of her uncertainty. "I'm looking forward to that."

"It's not easy to see it, but it *will* happen. I have faith that it will."

Sophie picked up her charts and started to do her rounds of the patients she was in charge of. Reagan let out an exhausted sigh and headed over to Peter's incubator.

She lifted the blanket that covered him and a smile crept across her face. There was a brief sense of relief to see him stable.

But she didn't know what to do.

Not that she could do much when he was at this critical point in his life.

He was stable. Sophie wasn't hovering currently. Sophie was doing her rounds and Peter was just lying there. All she wanted to do was hold him, but she didn't want to stress him by picking him up.

So she just stood there, watching him, feeling absolutely useless and helpless at the same time. She'd felt this way before, but usually when he was ill and she wasn't sure he was going to make

it, when she didn't have time to ponder these thoughts. To let them really sink in.

Now she did, and Reagan didn't like it very much. But she couldn't think that way or she'd go mad.

There was a tap on her shoulder and it was Kainan.

You left, he signed.

"I'm sorry. I didn't realize that I had…" she lowered her voice to a whisper, heat blooming in her cheeks "…spent the night."

Why are you whispering? Everyone knows that we've once spent the night together before. The evidence is right in front of us.

There was a mischievous twinkle in his eye and he grinned.

Reagan chuckled. "Sorry."

Don't apologize. You didn't leave a note or anything and I was worried.

"You were worried?" she asked, shocked.

Of course. I went to sleep with you there beside me and I woke up and you were gone.

"Sorry, I should've left a note."

Yes, he signed gently, and then his gaze drifted down to Peter and she could see hesitation in his eyes.

It stung.

She'd thought he cared for Peter. His hesitation now worried her. She didn't want Peter to be rejected by his father the way she'd been rejected by hers. That rejection had caused loathing in her mother, and Reagan knew her mother blamed her for her husband's distance.

"How did you know where I was?"

Andreas told me.

Then he frowned and pursed his lips together, as if he hadn't meant to sign that. As if it were a slip-up.

"Who is Andreas?" Reagan asked, confused.

The man in the next suite. He saw you this morning when you snuck out.

"Oh." For some reason she didn't quite believe Kainan. There was something he wasn't saying.

Once he said you'd snuck out I put two and two together and knew where you'd be.

"Of course." She sighed.

Kainan frowned. *What's wrong?*

"Nothing." She couldn't look at him right now. He wasn't telling her the truth and she was having a hard time trusting him. "What time is it?"

Almost ten. Are you ready to meet the medical students?

"No, but I suppose we must. We put them off

yesterday when I was called into surgery." She smiled the fake smile she'd mastered. "Are you ready?"

Of course. He grinned.

There was a confident air about him. One she envied.

"Well, let's go, then."

Reagan waved at Sophie on her way out and Sophie nodded in response. Reagan would be in the hospital. There was no way she was going to leave Peter for another night.

"So this Andreas…" she started.

What about him? Kainan asked.

"He sounded Hermosian to me."

Kainan frowned. *What makes you say that?*

"I spent over a year in Isla Hermosa. He reminded me of someone, but I can't remember…"

Déjà vu, that's all. It's being around me. You think anyone with that type of accent is Hermosian, he signed, cutting her off.

He was annoyed.

"Why are you getting so angry?"

I'm not angry.

"You're being very touchy about it."

I don't know where Andreas is from. He arrived

at the hotel with some coworkers around the same time I did and we've met in the hall a few times. Can we just drop it?

"Sure."

And she should. She didn't want to get involved with him. Peter was her priority. The only problem with that was that Kainan was Peter's father.

She couldn't lock Kainan out. For the sake of Peter she had to care, had to be involved and let Kainan in.

Plus you cared for him once.

Yes, she had, but that felt like a lifetime ago. They'd both been very different people back then.

"Good." He said the word out loud and then cleared his throat, interrupting her thoughts.

It was apparent that he was still annoyed about the course their conversation had taken, and for some reason Reagan couldn't help but wonder if he was hiding something about Andreas. And, if he was, why?

It's not your concern.

But Reagan knew when people were lying, and she had the gut feeling that Kainan was lying to her.

The question was why.

Who cares?

And that thought made her force those doubts from her mind. She really didn't have time for this. What Kainan did was his own business. She didn't have time to form a relationship with Kainan outside the bond of their son and their professional relationship. All she had time for was her son.

That was all that mattered.

Kainan opened the door to the lecture hall that was inside the hospital and gestured for her to take the lead.

Right now she had to focus on translating the American Sign Language for the medical students in this room. This was her new assignment. She was here to work with Kainan and that was it. Her feelings with respect to Kainan couldn't be allowed to come into play.

She had to keep reminding herself of that fact.

When Kainan had been able to speak, and before civil war had torn his country to shreds, he'd been at the forefront of surgery. He'd been on a fast track to win a Nobel Prize in medicine for his surgical advances.

AMY RUTTAN 109

Of course then his father had died and his
brother had taken over. He hadn't even lasted a
year and then everything had gone to heck.

One of the perks of working here in this hospi-
tal in Toronto, while waiting for surgery to cor-
rect his voice, was being able to continue with his
medical research. He was looking forward to that.

That was, of course, if he could train his medi-
cal students in triage in time to work on his re-
search. It had been a long time since he'd taught.
And he wasn't sure he had the patience for it.

Of course with Reagan by his side it would be
a snap. Not only because she would be able to
help him communicate with these eager medical
students, but because when they had worked to-
gether in the field, in the mobile military hospi-
tal, everything had just seemed to flow.

And as he worked with her now, guiding his stu-
dents through triage in a mock active war zone,
he was happy to be with her again.

He'd forgotten how well they worked together.
Two surgeons from two different countries, dif-
ferent backgrounds, but they came together seam-
lessly to create perfection.

Just like Peter.

His heart swelled with pride for a brief moment as he thought of the beautiful boy who was clinging to life in the pediatric critical care unit.

Everything was right when he was with Reagan. It thrilled him, but terrified him just the same.

If his brother were still King, then he would be jumping into the fray with her, begging her to stay with him. But now that *he* was King he didn't have his own life, and he hated the thought of ruining her life too. As much as he loved his country, he hated being King. He hated the shackles, the restrictions it entailed.

It was tearing him up inside. Just as it had destroyed his mother. And although Reagan was strong, she was vulnerable, and he didn't want to hurt her or overtax her.

"Mother, why are you so sad?" he'd asked once, when his mother had barely looked at him.

She'd put her arm around his shoulders as she'd sighed, looking out at the sea.

"I want to be free, Kainan."

"You are free. You are the Queen."

"I know."

Kainan turned his focus back on the students.

This was his task now. He couldn't let memories distract him.

"Good," he said, to a student who was performing a very complicated stitch with makeshift tools.

"Thank you, Dr. Laskaris." The student was beaming.

Kainan nodded and moved on.

As he walked the room, watching Reagan showing a couple of medical students a technique for draping with plastic, he saw Andreas out of the corner of his eye, standing outside the window of the lecture hall where they were with the medical students.

Kainan's stomach dropped to the soles of his feet.

There was a determined look about Andreas. Kainan had known Andreas for some time, and he knew when his head of security was stressed. And Andreas was stressed now.

Kainan darted out of the room. Reagan called after him, but he ignored her as he caught up to Andreas.

"The press know," Andreas said, not mincing his words. "I do not know who leaked it, Your

Majesty. The press are outside the hotel and in the avenue below us..."

Are they here in the hospital?

Andreas pursed his lips together and nodded.

Dammit.

Kainan raked his hand through his hair. He was enraged that he'd been discovered, and if he found out who had sold him out he was going to ignore his Hippocratic Oath and do horrible things to that individual.

"Kainan, what's...?" Reagan trailed off as she looked at Andreas closely, and she wasn't just recognizing him from this morning either.

Kainan's heart skipped a beat, because Andreas had been a soldier as well as a bodyguard during the Hermosian civil war. Andreas had been injured and Reagan had been the one to aid him.

And, by the way Reagan looked at Andreas now, she was picturing him with his head shaved, instead of with the long dark hair that Andreas now sported.

"I know you," she whispered.

"Of course—we met this morning," Andreas said, trying to bluff it out.

Reagan shook her head. "No, you were a sol-

dier. I treated you. I remember you with shorter hair and you...you are Hermosian."

Andreas looked worried and sent Kainan a look, which Reagan caught.

"What's going on?" she asked, her voice rising. "And don't get annoyed with me, Kainan. I *know* something is going on. There's something you're not telling me."

Let me explain, Reagan, Kainan signed, and scrubbed his hand over his face.

He saw that Michael McNeil, the Chief of Surgery, was rushing toward them.

"Dr. Laskaris—a word!"

Reagan frowned. "Michael? Are you okay?"

"No," Michael said hurriedly, and then he crossed his arms, looking directly at Kainan. "I have press surrounding my hospital."

"Press?" Reagan asked.

"Yes, and they're blocking the ambulance bay. I have all my security guards trying to keep them out, but how do you keep people out of a hospital?" Michael looked annoyed. "Dr. Laskaris, they're looking for *you*!"

Kainan's stomach knotted. He was angry, but

he felt defeated, because there was no sense in hiding now.

He'd been found. Even though he'd been trying to keep a low profile until after his surgery, when he hoped he'd have a voice again.

Reagan looked confused. "Kainan, what's going on?"

Andreas cleared his throat and Michael stood behind Reagan, his hands on his hips, looking just as confused as she was.

Kainan took a deep breath and mustered all his strength to whisper breathlessly, "I am the lost King of Isla Hermosa."

CHAPTER FIVE

"YOU'RE...WHAT?" REAGAN ASKED, not sure that she'd heard Kainan correctly. "You're a king? The Hermosian King? I thought he died?"

Kainan sighed and turned to look away.

"Dr. Laskaris?" Michael asked.

Andreas stepped forward. "He became King when his brother King Aleksander the Seventh died after an explosion in the palace. As you're all aware, King Aleksander's rule was tenuous, at best..."

Kainan spun back round, and there was a fire in his dark eyes that scared her.

I am King. My brother is dead and I am the missing King, he signed.

Reagan frowned. "The name Laskaris isn't associated with the Hermosian crown, and you told me when we first met that your family was from Greece."

Kainan sighed. *My mother was born in Greece.*

Isla Hermosa was founded by the Spanish and the Greeks. The name Laskaris is tied to the Hermosian crown, but it is kept for the "spares." Like me. I didn't want to change it when I became King. I am still Dr. Laskaris.

There was a sadness to his expression which softened her a bit. It was apparent that he wasn't happy with his new position in his country.

"You *were* injured in an IED blast?" Reagan asked. "At the front?"

Yes. I was injured trying to save my brother, but that was for nothing. He died after the explosion. I am the last of my line, so the Canadian government thought it prudent to take me away from my country. They brought me here, where I recuperated, and now I wait for surgery. I cannot sit idly by and do nothing. But it is not safe for me to go back yet.

Reagan nodded, but it was hard to take it all in.

Why hadn't he told her that he was a prince when they were working together? She'd thought he was just a surgeon.

But had they ever really talked about personal stuff?

No, they hadn't. Not ever.

It explained why Kainan had that air of command about him. Why other people in the Hermosian Army and the wounded civilians had been in such awe of him. He'd been a prince and she'd been too blind or naive to see it.

Another scary thought sank into her mind. If Kainan was King that meant Peter was a prince.

Peter might not be able to stay with her if it came to a custody fight. Even at his tender age Peter had a duty to the country of his father's birth. He belonged to Isla Hermosa.

Not to her.

As if sensing her apprehension, Kainan signed, *This changes nothing. Peter is your son. I will not take him from you.*

She wanted to believe him, but she was having a hard time processing all this.

"I'm surprised that your brother allowed you to serve as a doctor in a field hospital," she said, because she didn't know what else to say. She didn't know of many surgeon kings.

My late brother didn't care much for me. I was only the spare. Kainan turned to Andreas. *Please help Dr. McNeil deal with this security situation.*

Andreas bowed deeply. "Yes, Your Majesty."

Michael and Andreas walked away. Kainan turned to her, pain etched across his face.

I am sorry, Reagan. I could tell no one. Not until I'd had the surgery. Canada needs to protect me until my coronation.

"When is that? When is your coronation?"

New Year's Day.

"And your surgery?"

The twenty-sixth of this month. It's risky.

"How risky?"

With the severe amount of scar tissue...

He frowned and her heart sank. She knew.

"It's bad, then?"

Yes.

She nodded, but still the reality of it all was not sinking in. "That day at the palace..."

I tried to save Alek, but Alek wouldn't leave. The fool thought I wanted to be King.

"Why would he think that?" she asked.

My brother was a fool. The IED went off as I was trying to get him out of the palace and he didn't survive his injuries. So here I stand. King of Isla Hermosa. A voiceless king.

"I don't know what..." She trailed off as she thought about Peter upstairs. The sense of dread

was threatening to drown her. The thought of the press pushing their way into Peter's room was too horrible to think about. "Do the press know about Peter?"

Kainan shook his head. *No, they do not. They do not know about you or Peter, and I plan to keep it that way to protect you both.*

She nodded, but she wasn't sure that he would be able to. She wasn't sure about anything, and she didn't even really know him anymore.

Reagan had thought that Kainan was just a simple Hermosian surgeon. Nobody famous, just a person who tried to save lives, like her. But instead he'd been living this whole double life when they were on the island.

He was a king. Kainan might have called himself the "spare," but he was still royalty. It was a little too much to take in at the moment.

No wonder there was so much security surrounding Kainan at the Royal York. No wonder the Canadian government had insisted that Kainan come here, Dr. Shaw was one of the best otolaryngologists in the country. It also explained why he was being put up in such an opulent hotel.

Kainan was being protected.

"Dr. Laskaris, Dr. Cote…what should we do now?" asked a medical student.

Reagan and Kainan both spun round to see a few of the medical students in the doorway. A couple of them were staring at Kainan with wide-eyed awe.

These students must have heard about the civil war that had ripped the island nation of Isla Hermosa apart. How the late King Aleksander had been a tyrant and driven the country's resources into the ground. As well as cutting off a lot of trade and manufacturing, King Alek had been an ill-informed, misguided playboy who had cost a lot of lives.

And they probably all knew about the missing King too.

The missing King who was standing in front of her. Who was the father of her baby.

At least the press doesn't know about Peter, and we have to keep it that way.

"Why don't you head back to the university? Class is dismissed for today," Reagan said, making an executive decision.

The students turned back into the room to gather

up their stuff and Reagan started to walk away, because she needed to let all this sink in.

Kainan caught up with her as she headed down a quiet hallway that was rarely used. The beds on that wing were closed, and she needed the peace of the closed ward to regain her composure. But she had a feeling that was not going to happen, because Kainan had followed her and insisted on signing.

I meant what I said. This changes nothing, Reagan. My being King changes nothing about this situation. We're in Canada. We're not in Isla Hermosa.

She wanted to believe him, but she couldn't.

It's Kainan, a little voice said, but that didn't matter anymore. She didn't know him. Not really. The man she'd thought she knew didn't really exist. He was a stranger.

Nothing changes, he reiterated.

"Oh, really?"

"I am still me," he whispered breathlessly.

"I don't know who that is." She stopped to face him. "I never really knew you. We spent all that time together, working side by side, but we were strangers."

Kainan scrubbed a hand over his face. *I couldn't tell you I was spare to the heir. Do you know how many women found out who I was and immediately changed. They just wanted my wealth. They wanted status. With you I could just be me.*

"You *knew* I wasn't like that."

In the end, yes, I did. But you can understand my hesitation. At the beginning I knew nothing about you either.

Reagan thought about this, then nodded. "How many women are we talking about?" she asked, trying to ease the tension a little.

Kainan smiled. *Okay, not that many. When women found out who I was they pursued me. I wasn't the playboy my brother was.*

"I just wish you had told me."

What would telling the truth have done? Nothing. We were at war. I don't think of myself as a leader. I wasn't trained to step into my father's shoes. All I ever wanted to be was a surgeon, and it was refreshing to be just that when we were working together.

"What does this mean for our son?"

Nothing at the moment. He is illegitimate.

Her eyes widened at his words. *Nothing at the moment.* What did he mean by that?

Despite what he'd said about nothing changing, did he mean to legitimize Peter and take him away? And then she recalled what legitimizing meant to a royal. It meant marriage. And if it meant what she thought it meant, she would need more than a moment. She would need a lifetime.

There was no way she was going to marry Kainan just because they had a son together—just because they'd once had feelings for each other and had had a great night of sex.

That was not something to base a marriage on. Her parents had married for that, and her mother had resented her for pushing her father away. First of all because he'd wanted a son and then because he'd thought Reagan was a burden, cramping his lifestyle.

Reagan didn't want a marriage like that.

She never wanted to get married.

"At the moment?" she asked, trying not stumble over the words.

If we marry...

Reagan began to laugh at the absurdity of it all. "No, I don't think so."

Kainan's dark eyes narrowed. *I didn't ask you.*

"I'm saving you the trouble. There's no way."

Reagan, he's my son too.

"I am very aware of that, *Your Majesty.* But just because he's your son it doesn't mean that I'm going to marry you. Just because you're King it doesn't mean that I want to marry you."

Kainan rolled his eyes. *This is exactly why I didn't tell you. You've changed.*

"I thought that was why you liked me—because I wasn't after your title or your money. I'm still not, by the way. I haven't changed."

You're more cynical.

"I have every right to be!"

Why? he asked.

She couldn't tell him. She didn't want to share with him or anyone her painful past. To do that would be letting him in, leaving her exposed.

Reagan softened. "I'm sorry. I can't marry you. I don't ever want to get married."

Kainan nodded and then took a step closer to her. *Are you saying you never cared for me in that way?*

"I cared for you, Kainan. It just feels like a life-

time ago, and you are not the man I thought you were either."

And you would've turned me down back then?

He reached out and touched her cheek briefly, before signing again.

You would've turned down a proposal of marriage from me then? When I was the man you thought I was?

Yes. I would.

Only she didn't say it out loud. That was for her only.

"We were friends. Did you really want to propose to me back then?" she asked, but her pulse was racing.

His simple touch still affected her and she recalled the moment when he'd finally taken her in his arms and kissed her.

She remembered it with vivid clarity. The sweltering heat, the sound of the waves crashing against the shore and all the chaos that had seemed to still around them in that moment.

"If things had been different..." Kainan whispered, then stroked her cheek again.

His arm slipped around her as he tipped up her chin and captured her lips in a kiss. She closed

her eyes and drank it in. This stolen moment that took her right back to that time.

And even though she didn't want to feel this way about him, because she didn't have an inch of her heart to give him, she couldn't help but be swept away.

It was like a dream.

All those months when she'd thought he was dead, and right now he was a reality.

He was here.

Alive and kissing her.

He was affecting her, bringing down her walls. She couldn't let him in.

She pushed him away. "Kainan, it doesn't change anything. I never want to marry. Royalty or not, it doesn't change how I feel about marriage."

Reagan, I can take care of you and Peter.

"How?" she asked. "You can't give him a new heart by making him a prince."

He looked crestfallen. *I can protect you both.*

"From what?"

Those who wish to end the monarchy of Isla Hermosa.

She frowned. "But you said it yourself—he's

not legitimate so he's not a threat. If I marry you so you can protect us, I'm actually endangering us further."

Kainan's shoulders slumped. *You'd still be a target if people found out. I am sorry. I just... I want to protect you both. I haven't done much for you, but I can do that. Let me do this. It's the right thing to do.*

She reached out and grabbed his hand. "Being here now is enough, but we need to protect Peter. His last name is Cote, not Laskaris. The only people who know that you're his father are the pediatric critical care unit staff and Michael. They won't say a word."

My security team knows.

Reagan's stomach knotted. "You'll have to keep them away from him. They'll attract attention."

He pursed his lips together, annoyed. *I will not call them off. I don't even think that I can anyway. They're protecting the monarchy of Isla Hermosa.*

"Then the press will find out."

Security will keep them out of the hospital.

Reagan rolled her eyes. "Don't underestimate the press."

Fine. They will keep their distance. But the mo-

ment something happens to you or Peter I am bringing about the security detachment in force.

"Deal." She held out her hand to shake his.

Kainan didn't take it. *I'm going to check in with Andreas and make sure that everything is good.*

"Okay. I'm going to check on Peter and then see if they need any help in the emergency department, since we sent the medical students home early."

I want you to have dinner with me tonight.

"How is that keeping your distance, Kainan? Won't the press see me having dinner with you?"

Not if you come to my hotel room. No one will notice you and my guards can provide a distraction.

Reagan crossed her arms. "Why do you want me to have dinner with you?"

Kainan pinched the bridge of his nose. *Why must you question everything?*

"I'm not leaving the hospital tonight, Kainan. I shouldn't have left yesterday. I'm needed here."

To do what? Peter is stable.

"I'm not leaving. So, no, I'm not having dinner with you tonight."

Fine, but I'm not giving up on this.

Kainan walked away and Reagan shook her head. She knew he was stubborn enough that he would persist until she agreed, but she wasn't going to leave the hospital tonight.

She was going to stay right by Peter.

With this threat of the press, and people who would do harm to Kainan, she was going to make sure that no one got to Peter.

Kainan waited outside the pediatric critical care unit. He didn't want to go in on the off-chance that someone from the press had snuck inside. It was killing him not to see Peter, but this was for the best.

Until he could make Reagan his wife and legitimize Peter he had to keep his distance from his son. Only he didn't want to. He didn't want to be like his father, a distant, remote figure.

If the press found out about Peter then all hell would break loose. Yet Kainan had to legitimize him. He had to marry Reagan and provide for them both. It was the right thing to do.

He saw Reagan walking toward the pediatric critical care unit, her head down and rubbing her neck. She looked tired and he didn't blame her.

He needed to do more. Reagan needed help, even if she didn't trust him.

He had heard from Sophie that Reagan had spent every night since Peter was born watching him. Except for last night. She hadn't even had a chance to recover much from the birth. She was always there, beside Peter.

One night of sleep would not make up for all the nights she'd lost. All the time she hadn't taken to heal. All the weight she had on her shoulders.

Kainan wanted to help her because the guilt of not being there for her was eating away at him like so many things did, but this was more real. This was a weight that he would gladly bear, that he *wanted* to bear for her.

"Reagan." He said her name uncertainly, because he wasn't sure his voice would be able to say it in a way for her to hear him.

She stopped and looked up. "Kainan—I thought you had returned to the hotel. Your security detachment isn't here."

Not that you can see. They're always around.

Reagan gave him a halfhearted smile. "What're you still doing here? I told you I didn't want to have dinner."

I know, but you do have to eat sometime.

"I'm not leaving the hospital, Kainan. I told you that."

I know, and that is why I have arranged for dinner in the classroom.

"What?" she asked, raising a finely arched brow.

It's cafeteria food, and I know that you said yesterday that you were tired of cafeteria food, but seeing how you won't leave the hospital, and I don't want to draw attention, I didn't really have a choice.

She crossed her arms, a smile spread across her face. "You *are* persistent."

I may be King now, but I haven't changed that much.

"Is a king supposed to change?" she teased.

I don't know.

They both laughed at that.

Come on, he's stable. He's fine right now. Eat first, and then you can man your post by his bedside, or I can man the post and you can sleep in a proper bed.

"You want to take a shift by Peter's bedside?" she asked, surprised. As if she didn't quite believe him or the help he was offering.

Yes.

"You? Shouldn't you be resting before your surgery?"

That's not for a few days yet. Let me take a shift. I want to do it.

"I don't know…"

She looked over her shoulder at the door of the pediatric critical care unit and he knew the pull she was feeling. He was feeling it too.

It was hard not to when your child was lying there sick.

You are no good to him weakened. You need to eat, Reagan. Come.

Reagan tore her glance away and nodded. "You're right."

Of course I am. I am King, after all.

It was a tease, and Reagan rolled her eyes, but she laughed all the same.

"Lead the way, my liege."

I'm not your liege, Reagan. You are not Hermosian. He held out his arm. *However, I am a gentleman, so if you'll do me the honor and let me escort you?*

Reagan took his arm and they walked away from the pediatric critical care unit to the class-

room that was at the far end of the hall, on the other side of the hospital.

They didn't say anything. It was night, and the hospital was quiet. All the regular appointments and coming and goings that happened during the day, making the hospital a busy place, were gone. There were a few staff members walking past, because the emergency room never stopped running, but for the most part the hospital was deserted.

The lighting was low and it was very calm. The cafeteria was only serving coffee and sandwiches. The gift shop was closed and through the atrium window he could see snow falling softly.

In a couple of days it would be Christmas, then his surgery, and then New Year's, which would be his coronation.

If he survived the surgery and *if* the surgery was successful.

Kainan couldn't remember the last time he'd celebrated Christmas. He'd always made excuses to his father in order to avoid the holiday since his mother had died. So for years, he hadn't celebrated it. He'd worked and he'd enjoyed that.

And then war had broken out.

He'd spent last Christmas with Reagan, in the

mobile military hospital. She had sung Christmas carols to the soldiers. Just thinking about that made him smile.

"What're you smiling about?" she asked.

I was thinking about last Christmas with you.

She smiled. "I remember that night."

You brought a lot of hope to those wounded soldiers.

"It was Christmas—it's all about hope. Although I wouldn't really know…"

Did you not celebrate Christmas as a child?

"No. Well, sort of. My parents never really liked to spend time with me. I had a grandmother until I was about seven, who made the holiday special, but after she died my parents were very cold to me. They didn't want me and they made it clear."

He frowned. *I'm sorry, and I can understand that.*

"You understand? I thought your father was a great king?"

Yes—a great king, but a very cold, detached father. I was the spare, so he didn't spend a lot of time with me. Besides, Christmas was all pomp and circumstance. It was all for show.

"Sounds like we both had it rough," she whispered. "Still, Christmas is a time for hope."

Do you feel hopeful about this Christmas?

The wistful smile disappeared, to be replaced with sigh. "I'm trying, but it's hard. This is Peter's first Christmas and he's spending it here."

Kainan understood. He wished it was different. *At least he's still alive.*

She smiled at him, her eyes glistening. "Yes. He is."

Kainan opened the door to the classroom, where he'd set up a small dining area. He'd borrowed plates and cutlery from the cafeteria, with Andreas's help. He only wished there were candl or something, so he could set some mood li ing, but candles weren't allowed in the ho He wanted to make it special to her.

He pulled out a seat and beckoned fo sit. Once she'd sat down he pushed he and then took the seat next to her. The tab too long, and he didn't want her to have to sh across the room. This way, if he wanted to speak to her then he wouldn't have to shout.

He longed to speak to her as he'd used to be able to do. With his voice he could offer to hold her hand, touch her and comfort her.

At least she could understand him, though. Not many people knew how to use American Sign

Language. He had learned it in medical school, because he'd wanted to converse with hearing impaired or nonverbal patients in his medical practice. He'd had no idea that it would become a part of his life.

"What's for dinner?" she asked.

Kainan lifted the lids on the salads he'd ordered before the cafeteria had shut down. *I believe it is called Cobb Salad.*

"It looks good. Actually, the cafeteria makes a great Cobb salad."

Well, this is just the starter. The main course is ̶oni and cheese. I can't say that I've had the ̶re of trying macaroni and cheese.

̶'re pulling my leg," Reagan said.

̶true. It's not really a staple on Isla Her- ̶ and I grew up in a palace with a team of ̶ks. Macaroni and cheese wasn't in their repertoire.*

"Then you missed out, my friend," she teased.

He chuckled. *I took a peek at it. I highly doubt that.*

Reagan smiled brightly, her dark eyes twinkling under the fluorescent lighting.

You have beautiful smile, Reagan.

Pink crept up her neck into her cheeks. "You've told me that before."

It's the truth.

"Why are you doing this?" she asked.

Doing what?

"This dinner. Why?"

I'm doing this because I wasn't there for you when Peter was born. I see the burden you carry and I want to help. Don't be on the defensive so much. You can trust me.

She looked away. "It's dangerous for you to help right now."

I know, but at least I can do this. I may not be able to directly help him, but I can help make things easier for you.

Her spine stiffened a bit. "I don't need help. I got myself into this situation and I can handle it."

I believe I was part of this "situation", as you call it. Unless Peter was another immaculate conception, I had a hand in helping you.

Reagan sighed and relaxed. "Okay, thank you for dinner. I appreciate it."

Kainan nodded. *Eat. You need to eat to keep your strength up. You're no good to our son if you get sick or collapse from exhaustion.*

Reagan nodded and they ate in silence, but it wasn't awkward. It felt right, and it was nice just to sit there with her and enjoy the peace and quiet, alone in this section of the hospital.

When they'd finished, Reagan leaned back in her chair. "That was good. What did you think of the macaroni and cheese?"

It was...interesting.

He made a face and she laughed, then she picked up her phone and frowned.

What's wrong? Kainan asked when she looked up again.

"It's Peter. His stats are a bit low." She bit her lip and then got up. "I have to be with him."

Kainan nodded. *Go and keep me posted. Please.*

Her expression softened. "I will. Thank you for dinner. I really appreciate it."

He nodded and she left the room.

Kainan sank back in the office chair he was been sitting in, spinning a bit as he tried not to think about what was happening to his son, or the fact that he was helpless. It was too much to bear.

He had to marry Reagan to protect her, to protect them both—especially if he didn't survive the surgery. Although he was very aware that he

would be ruining her life *and* Peter's by staying and subjecting them to royal protocol.

He should just walk away. Only he couldn't. And the fact that he couldn't scared him.

CHAPTER SIX

IT HAD BEEN a couple days since their impromptu dinner that night in the classroom. It was the nicest thing that anyone had ever done for her in a long time. Actually, Reagan couldn't remember the last time someone had done something so nice for her.

Maybe there was still a piece of the man she'd thought she knew in there. Kainan had promised her nothing would change with respect to Peter. He wouldn't try and take him away.

Could she believe him?

She sighed, hating the doubt that still crept in.

He had been trying really hard, but since that dinner he had kept his distance both from her and Peter. It broke her heart to see him keeping Peter at arm's length, especially when Peter wasn't doing particularly well at the moment.

You asked him to stay away, remember?

And she had. He was doing what she'd asked.

It had been to keep Peter safe. Now she wasn't so sure that it had been the right decision.

Peter needed both his parents, and Kainan was alive. It was a miracle, and she shouldn't keep Kainan away from Peter or vice versa, but there was danger attached to Kainan and that made her fear for her son. She feared Peter might be hurt when Kainan returned to Isla Hermosa.

It was across the Atlantic. If Kainan had meant what he'd said about not trying to take her son away from her, Peter wouldn't see Kainan much. As King, Kainan's duties would take over—and what would happen when he married?

A king needed a queen.

You could be that queen.

No, she couldn't. Her life was here.

What life?

Still, she was protecting Peter's heart. She didn't want him to feel abandonment as she had. It was the right decision that he stayed away, so the press wouldn't discover Peter. News of Kainan's presence in Toronto was in all the papers. Not that she'd had a lot of time to read in between her duties at the hospital and being with Peter.

All she'd had time for was the headlines.

The world was waiting for Kainan to say something. Anything. Yet he couldn't. Not until after his surgery.

Reagan knew that Michael was overwhelmed in keeping the press out of the hospital so that they didn't pry into Kainan's life. Or hers.

At least there had been no mention of her. Which meant they didn't know about Peter.

That was good, but who knew how long that would last? It was something she didn't want to think about it.

She watched Kainan now, from a distance. He was sitting in the empty classroom, writing. When they'd served in Isla Hermosa he had told her that he was at the forefront of a new surgical technique that would save lives, but the war had put an end to that.

He was researching again now, while the medical students were on a break for the upcoming Christmas holidays. That meant Kainan didn't really need Reagan unless he was out and about in the hospital. Although she couldn't help but wonder how he would be able to develop a surgical technique when he couldn't speak.

To develop a surgical technique he had to be

able to perform surgery, and without his voice that was something he couldn't do at the moment.

She was impressed by him. He was so strong. That was what had drawn her in last time. She smiled to herself, still watching Kainan. How did he get to her? Especially when no one else did.

It was thrilling, but unnerving. Those walls of hers had protected her for so long, and yet Kainan could get through to her.

"You do remember me, don't you, Dr. Cote?"

Reagan spun around to see a security guard— the one who had spoken to her in the hallway at the Royal York. The one she remembered working on in the field. Kainan's security guard—Andreas.

"I do. It took me some time. I wasn't used to seeing you with hair."

The security guard smiled. "I prefer this length over the required shaved head for military service. His Majesty does not care if I keep my hair long, as long as it doesn't interfere in my duties."

"I'm sorry I didn't recognize you right away, sir," she said sheepishly.

He smiled gently. "It's Andreas—and do not worry. I suspect you have a lot on your mind, especially in regard to your son being so ill."

Reagan nodded. "I appreciate the fact you're keeping an eye on him. He's not Hermosian…"

"He may not have been born there, but he is still half-Hermosian. He is heir to the throne—that's if he is legitimized." There was hope in his eyes as he looked her.

She chuckled nervously. "Right…"

That wasn't going to happen, but Andreas didn't need to know that.

"I thank you for saving my life that night and for singing me those Christmas songs. I have never forgotten that moment."

Reagan smiled. "I was just doing my duty—as were you. There is no need to thank me."

Andreas dipped his head. "Ah, but you sang so sweetly. It gave me such hope. You *still* give me hope."

Warmth flooded her cheeks and she discovered she didn't like the attention he was lavishing on her. "How do you mean?"

Andreas opened his mouth to say something further, and then looked over her shoulder and froze. "My apologies. I must get back to my duties."

Reagan turned to see that Kainan was standing

in the doorway. His hands were in his pockets and he was glaring at Andreas. It was an expression that meant business. It caused a shiver to go down her spine.

Andreas skulked away and Kainan's gaze never left his retreating form. He looked like a true king—or at least like the ones she'd seen depicted in movies.

"That was rude," Reagan snapped. King or not, she didn't like it when people treated others badly.

He was treading where he should not, Kainan signed, and mouthed a curse word.

"What're you talking about?"

There are affairs of my kingdom that do not concern you. You do not need to know about them.

"Okay..."

And he does not need to know our personal business.

"I agree," she said, relieved.

Kainan's expression softened. *How are you? I have not seen you these last couple of days.*

"I've been busy. Actually, I'm on my way to see Peter's pediatrician in his office. I came to see if you wanted to come."

Kainan frowned. *What's wrong?*

Reagan sighed. "Peter hasn't been doing so well and the doctor wants to touch base."

His brow furrowed and she could tell that something was bothering him.

Does this doctor know who I am?

"That you're his father and the King of Isla Hermosa? Yes, he knows, and he's signed the confidentiality agreement that Michael has forced upon all those dealing with our special situation."

Kainan let out a sigh, relief on his face. *Then I would like to go and hear for myself.*

"Okay."

Kainan hesitated. *That's if you want me to go?*

"I wouldn't have offered if I didn't."

I have been staying away, like you asked.

Her stomach flip-flopped with guilt. "I know, but perhaps I was wrong."

He cocked an eyebrow.

"Yes, I was wrong. Don't stay away."

She was afraid Kainan that would leave, and that would hurt Peter, but Peter not knowing his father at all and growing up to learn that Reagan had kept Kainan away would be worse.

Peter needed Kainan.

Kainan smiled, those dark eyes twinkling as his gaze held her captive. *Then I won't.*

"Good."

Kainan locked up the classroom and they headed toward the pediatric wing of the hospital, where Dr. Braccio worked.

Reagan sighed. "You know, I sometimes wonder if I would have been better off without my parents."

Why is that? Kainan signed.

"They never wanted me. Their resentment was horrible. I wouldn't wish that on anyone."

You had no love?

"Did you? You said your father wasn't the best."

Yes, but my mother loved me. He smiled wistfully. *So I was lucky.*

"I'm glad you're here, Kainan. Peter needs you. He needs both of us. I didn't have my parents when I really needed them and…it was miserable. You're here, alive, and Peter should have every opportunity to get to know you."

Kainan nodded. *Thank you. I want to get to know him too…before I have to return to Isla Hermosa.*

Her stomach clenched. "You have a country to run."

Let me worry about that. You know I will be there for Peter if he needs me. Of course I could be there all the time if—

She knew where he was going and she didn't want to go there.

"How is the research coming?" she interrupted, changing the subject but feeling the awkward tension that was between them suddenly.

Good. I am glad to be working on it again. It was my one true passion. I never wanted to be a king. I just wanted medicine.

"I know—you've told me."

And what is your grand passion, besides our son?

"I don't know," she said. "I enjoyed my time in the military, and when I left Isla Hermosa I was excited to be working at this hospital in trauma. I guess I never really thought beyond those plans, because I found out I was pregnant and my focus shifted."

Come on, there must've been something?

"I once wanted to teach medicine," she admitted. "I wanted to teach at my alma mater."

Where was that?

"I went to medical school in London, Ontario.

It's a small city, about two hours west of here. I just loved London. Toronto is my hometown, but it's too big for me. The prices of the homes are astronomical here, but in London housing is a bit more affordable. I could actually buy a small house and Peter would have a yard to play in. Of course when Peter was born so ill I really had no choice. I had to stay here."

She laughed nervously.

"It's not as wild as your aspirations to win a Nobel prize for medicine or anything."

It's still a good aspiration. He smiled at her. *It's good to dream of something like that, because that sounds wonderful to me. I didn't have the luxury to go and play outside when I was a child.*

"Oh?" she asked.

Well, there were always threats when it came to the Young Princes. More so with Alek than me, but still... If I did get to go outside then I was followed by Security. There were a few times I managed to sneak away.

"And where did you sneak off to?" she asked with a smile.

To the ocean. I was fascinated by tidal pools and I liked to swim. My mother was terrified of

the ocean. Her brother was carried away by a rip tide and died when she was a young girl, so when she found out that I was sneaking away from my bodyguards and heading to the ocean to swim I got in a lot of trouble. I was shipped off to boarding school in Switzerland. Just mountains—no ocean.

"I'm sorry you didn't have freedom. I didn't have a huge amount of freedom growing up in the city. There wasn't many safe places to play—and forget about learning to ride a bike. I grew up on the Danforth."

What's the Danforth? Kainan asked.

"A part of Toronto—a neighborhood. It was busy, so I played in a shoebox-sized yard. My parents didn't really take me anywhere. We didn't travel. I think I was a bit of a burden to them."

He frowned. *Well, if it's any consolation I think I was a bit of a burden to my father too.*

"Not your mother, though?" she asked.

No, never my mother. Even though she died when I was ten. I was at boarding school when she got sick. I was brought back in time to say goodbye to her.

His expression softened and he had a faraway

look in his eyes, like the one he'd had the day before he'd been sent up to the front lines, when he had been staring at the smoke rising from the gates of Helicia.

"I'm sorry to hear that. How did she die?"

Cancer. She did not suffer long. All she wanted was her freedom... He sighed.

"Freedom? Was she a prisoner?"

In a way. She wasn't locked up, but a member of the royal family has to follow certain protocols, certain rules, and my mother was a bit of free spirit. He smiled sadly. *She loved my father, though he never really loved her. Not in the same way.*

Reagan could understand that. She'd often wondered if her parents really loved each other because they seemed so cold and so indifferent. She had never been quite sure that they were capable of love. At least Kainan had had love. His mother had loved him, and from the way Kainan described his mother it sounded as if he'd loved her too.

"I understand," she whispered.

You do? he signed, looking confused.

"My parents were very emotionally closed off

to me, and to each other. I didn't have the best childhood."

I'm sorry.

"I sometimes wonder if I can be the mother Peter needs." She blushed, annoyed with herself that she'd let that slip.

You're an excellent mother, Reagan.

Her pulse quickened as Kainan reached out and took her hand and they continued their walk to the pediatrician's office, moving in silence the rest of the way.

They stopped in front of Dr. Braccio's office and Reagan took a deep breath. She had a feeling about what Dan Braccio was going to tell her about Peter. She'd read his chart. Peter was dying. And time was running out for him to get a new heart.

Kainan, as if sensing her apprehension, gave her hand a squeeze and nodded with determination toward the door.

You can do this. You have to do this.

Reagan let go of Kainan's hand and knocked on the door.

Dan Braccio answered. "Reagan, come on in— and you must be Peter's father."

"Kainan," Kainan said carefully.

"Welcome—it's nice to meet you." Dan shook Kainan's hand, and as Reagan sat down on the edge of the chair Dan shut the door behind them, locking it so that no one would barge in.

Which was not a good sign.

Reagan's heart started to race and Kainan placed a hand on her shoulder to steady her, as if he knew that she was terrified.

"I'm glad you both could come, and I'm not going to mince words with you as you're doctors." Dan took a seat behind his desk. "Peter's cardio-myopathy is progressing rapidly."

"How long?" Reagan asked, her voice trembling slightly.

"A month, maybe, if we're lucky," Dan said sadly. "The pediatric cardiologist, Dr. Bruni, is very concerned."

Tears stung her eyes but she tried to keep it together. A month? That was it? That was all she'd have left with her son?

This couldn't be the end.

A year of life was all he got?

Her world was crumbling under her.

"He has been moved up the priority list on

UNOS," Dan said. "He's right at the top now. But you both know that infant hearts are hard to come by. I wanted him to get a bit older."

"He's three months old now—that's surely got to give him a better chance?"

Reagan was grasping at straws, but she wasn't ready to accept defeat yet. Not when it came to Peter. He was her whole world. She didn't have a contingency plan for life without him.

"Yes, I am glad he's not newborn. That does give us a slight advantage. It's easier to find an older heart for an infant as opposed to a newborn heart, but it's still difficult." Dan opened up Peter's file. "We do have a better shot now."

Kainan tapped her shoulder and she saw he was signing. Dan was watching and waiting for her to translate.

"Kainan would like to know the specifics of what will happen. Will he go on a left ventricular assist device?" she asked.

Dan nodded and looked at Kainan when he addressed him. "I would like to hook him up to an LVAD as soon as possible." He slid the consent form toward Reagan. "He's no stranger to surgery, but I hate having to do this to him…"

"I know," Reagan said dully. "But it's his only hope."

Dan nodded. "I'm sorry, Reagan and Kainan. I truly am. This is not an easy situation. I don't like delivering this kind of news."

Reagan didn't respond. What doctor *did* like delivering this kind of news? None that she could think of. But it was a part of the job and being on this end of the conversation sucked. Big-time.

It was as if someone was trying to cut her heart out with a blunt instrument and hand it to her while it was still beating.

If only she could give her heart to Peter she would. She would give up her life for him. Anything to have him live.

Reagan clicked the pen she didn't even remember picking up and signed her name on the form, dating it before sliding the form back to Dan.

"When will the surgery take place?" Reagan asked stonily. She was numb.

"As soon as possible. He needs to go on the device. I'm having my team and the cardiothoracic team prep him for surgery and ready everything I need. I hope to have his surgery done within the next couple of hours."

Reagan nodded. "Can I be with him?"

"Yes, but you won't be able to handle him. I'm sorry. We have to take every precaution to prevent infection. This will be taxing for him."

"I understand." Reagan stood. "Thank you, Dan."

Kainan went ahead of her and unlocked the door, holding it open for her. There were so many emotions rushing through her she wasn't sure what to do. Instead she bottled everything up tight.

There was no time for her to feel.

Right now she had to be strong for Peter.

Kainan seemed to understand. He said nothing, just walked beside her. This time he did not reach out to touch her and she was glad, because if he touched her she would lose it, and she didn't want to fall apart right now.

They gowned, gloved, and put on surgical masks before entering the pediatric critical care unit.

There were a few nurses and a couple of young pediatric surgical residents hovering around Peter's crib, and Reagan let out a hiss of pain and turned away. She couldn't stand to look.

Kainan's arm came around her and she looked up into his eyes.

"Be strong. You are strong," he whispered, his voice hoarse.

He winced, and she knew that uttering those words had been hard for him, painful as well. His words, his voice—even broken—gave her strength.

"I don't know if I'm *this* strong," she said, her voice cracking with the emotion that she could barely contain.

Kainan removed his arm and signed, *You've been here before. Peter needs you. He will pull through. This is his best chance.*

"I know." She turned back around and stood on the periphery, watching as they readied Peter for surgery. Sophie glanced up once from her work to nod briefly, and then turned back to Peter. Kainan stood beside her.

"I have never heard him cry," Reagan whispered urgently. "Well, not since the day he was born."

Kainan's expression was pained, but he said nothing.

"I would love to hear him cry again." Tears were

welling up in her eyes. "Just one more time. If I had a Christmas wish it would be that."

When he gets a new heart you will hear him cry all the time. It will probably drive you crazy.

Reagan smiled. "I would like that."

At least after the LVAD surgery you can hold him. In fact, it'll be encouraged. He'll need all your strength.

The surgical team came in and transferred her fragile son to a gurney, along with all his wires and tubes. He looked so small. She took a step forward, aching to reach out and touch him, but restrained herself.

"Touch him," Sophie whispered. "He needs you."

"I was told not to," Reagan said.

"Touch him. It's just a touch," Sophie encouraged.

Reagan nodded, tears rolling down her cheeks as she bent over her sick boy and touched his head through her rubber glove, kissing the soft skin that she'd never got to touch through the surgical mask.

"I'll be waiting," Reagan whispered. "Right here."

Kainan stepped forward, but then he hesitated and turned away, shaking his head. He couldn't do it, and it hurt her that he wouldn't reach out to touch their son, but she saw the pained expression on his face and understood.

She knew that look of pain—she lived it every day.

The surgical team rolled him out of the pediatric critical care unit. Reagan followed them. She would follow the gurney until she could do so no longer. Until it entered the surgical floor, where she would not be able to follow because she was a parent in this moment, not a surgeon.

It was hard to stop at the double doors that closed off the surgical wing from the rest of the hospital, but she stopped and watched as they rolled Peter away.

She hated being in a patient's shoes. She hated being on this side of the door.

Kainan was beside her. "Come," he said.

Reagan shook her head. She wouldn't let him take her away. It was as if staring at those double doors would somehow protect Peter, somehow bring him back to her.

"Reagan," Kainan said more firmly.

"I'm not leaving."

Before she knew what was happening Kainan was scooping her up in his arms and carrying her away, in broad daylight.

"Are you crazy?" she screeched. "Put me down!"

Kainan didn't respond, and he wouldn't look at her as he carried her to a small exam room that was dark and unoccupied. He set her down and then shut the door, locking it, then pulling down the blinds.

"What do you think you're doing?" she yelled at him. "People could've seen—people probably *did* see, you maniac!"

Let it out, he signed.

"Let what out?"

Let it all out. You can't bottle up that emotion forever. Let it out. Stop locking your emotions away.

She just stared at him at first, because she was so stunned at what he was suggesting, and all she could hear was her mother's voice in her head.

"Honestly, Reagan. You're a big girl now. Stop crying. It's embarrassing. You can hold it together," her mother had hissed at her when she'd

cried over the fact her dog had died. "Big girls don't cry."

"I don't have anything to let out." Her voice trembled.

Reagan, you don't have to hide with me.

The moment she saw what he'd signed it was like a floodgate opening up. She broke down weeping, covering her face with her hands, and let it all out—every piece of raw emotion that she had been bottling up inside her since Peter had been born.

Kainan took her in his arms and she clung to him. He ran his hand over her head, but it was hard for him to do that with the bun she had in her hair.

Still, it was what she needed.

She needed to be held. Her body trembled as he held her, the pain washing through her. The strength in his arms calmed her.

"There was nothing you could've done," Kainan had said back then, gripping her by the shoulders and shaking her. "You did everything you could."

"I didn't. I didn't save his life. That's what I could've done and I couldn't even do that!"

"His injuries were too severe. He stepped in

the path of an IED. There was nothing anyone could've done, but you gave him comfort."

"Comfort?" She'd wiped away her tears.

"You held him and he passed away peacefully, knowing that he was safe and that he was without pain. You did all you could. In fact you did more. Not many surgeons in this military hospital would do the same."

He'd pulled her into his arms then, giving her a hug, holding her close so that she would calm down as she cried in his arms.

"He was so young," she'd whispered against his neck. "He didn't get a chance to live."

"Some never do." He'd tipped up her chin, those dark eyes so reassuring, so understanding, and she'd known that he also felt the pain she'd felt in that moment.

"You did everything you could. You were strong for him. You *are* strong."

Reagan looked up at Kainan now, longing to hear him say those same things.

He did say those words. You just didn't hear them.

She studied his face. There were a few more scars, some creases in his face from worry, and

some grey in his dark curls. It suited him. But those dark eyes were the same. They were reflecting back the pain that she was feeling.

Acting on the need to be close to him, she kissed him. And it was as if she had come home. His arms wrapped around her, pulling her tight against him as they kissed. How long had she dreamed of this moment but been thrown back into reality, remembering that he had died?

Only he hadn't died.

He was here with her. He was here with Peter.

And for one brief moment, as she sank into the kiss that eased her sorrow, her pain and her worry, she forgot about it all. She forgot that he was King, that their son was dying and that she had been alone for so long.

She finally broke off the kiss and laid her head against his chest as he ran his hands over her back. He was still holding her as they stood in silence. The only sound was her own breath and the steady rhythm of his heart under her ear.

They stayed together in that stolen moment of peace, comforting each other as their son fought for his life.

Then Kainan's hand stilled and he moved away, knocking her out of the peaceful reverie.

I'm sorry for carrying you away like that, but it was the only way, he signed.

"I know. I'm sorry I called you a maniac."

He smiled, a dimple forming in his cheek. *I'm used to it. You've called me worse things before.*

She frowned. "When?"

Your Majesty. He made a sarcastic face, as if to drive home the point that she had said it in a spiteful way.

"I'm sorry about that too."

He shrugged. *I deserved it.*

"Still, thank you for being here with me. Thank you for bringing me here."

I thought you would've learned by now not to bottle up your emotions so much. You were about to burst.

She nodded. "I know. Thank you for coming to my rescue again."

He smiled, his expression softening. *You're welcome.*

Warmth crept up her neck into her cheeks. "I'm sorry for kissing you as well."

Never be sorry for that.

His dark eyes glinted with the promise of something more. Something she knew all too well. And as much as she wanted that, she couldn't do it. She couldn't divide herself between Peter's care and Kainan. It would be too much to bear. Peter and work—that was all she could handle.

Work was the only thing that kept her sane. It was structured and, though it was never predictable, she knew what she was doing. She could detach herself emotionally from it.

Starting something up with Kainan was not the answer, because she knew that she would never be able to detach herself emotionally from him.

He was definitely *not* predictable, and she wasn't sure she could handle losing both Peter *and* Kainan.

The thought of losing them both scared her beyond all reason. And she wasn't prepared to invest in that.

CHAPTER SEVEN

THE SURGERY SEEMED to take an eternity.

Kainan had stayed in the hospital until he was certain that Peter had pulled through and been hooked up to the left ventricular assist device. He'd done it with flying colors. Then he'd gone with Reagan to the pediatric critical care unit, where Peter had been moved to an isolation room.

There was only enough room for the nurses and the doctors to navigate and one chair, which was where Reagan had curled up in her street clothes with a hospital gown over her. She'd looked completely uncomfortable, but Kainan hadn't been able to get her to budge.

There had been no place for him. So he'd left.

He had to put some distance between himself and the hospital anyway. He felt so helpless.

Ever since he'd become King and been whisked away to Canada he'd felt this way, but it came

into painful Technicolor how truly helpless he was when he gazed into the incubator at his son.

He was just like his father, who had been absent for most of his childhood. Kainan was following in his father's lead and he loathed himself.

You didn't even know Peter existed. That's why you weren't there, he told himself.

Only that didn't make him feel any better. Things had to change. He refused to be like his father. His father who hadn't taken care of his illegitimate children…his father who had broken his mother's heart and been distant with his legitimate children.

Kainan refused to force Peter into an unhappy childhood like he'd had.

He'd already missed so much. Three months of Peter's life. And if he didn't get a new heart soon Kainan would never know him. Never speak to him.

Reagan said he didn't cry, that she'd barely heard Peter's voice.

Just like me.

Peter had no voice but he was still here, fighting to live.

Reagan was strong. She would be able to handle

the burdens of royal life. He felt guilty for having to impose them upon her, but it was the only way to protect them if he died.

Remember how it broke your mother, though. How it hardened Alek and you.

He had almost lost it when he'd seen Reagan bend over Peter before they took him to surgery. She had bent down and whispered to him to be strong and she'd touched him, kissed him through the surgical mask.

It had alost been too much for him to take. It had taken all his strength to keep himself from breaking down.

Reagan had been so strong and he so weak in that moment. The thought of losing his son had too much for him to bear, but Reagan had needed him. He knew she liked to have walls up, not to show any weakness. But when she cracked he would swallow his worry, his sorrow, and step up to bear it for her.

He wanted to take Reagan and Peter's pain for them. To be better than his own father. If Kainan didn't survive his surgery, if Peter wasn't legitimized, then Kainan wouldn't be able to leave his

fortune to them. It was the only thing he could think of doing to protect them.

It had made him think back to that night on Isla Hermosa, when the chaos had died down after the rebel attack on the front lines. When his foolish brother had demanded that the youngest and most untrained of the Hermosian Army should advance.

And that boy who had been no more than eighteen had taken the brunt of the explosion. All they'd been able to do was patch him together, but they had known it wouldn't stop him from dying. That boy had been alone and dying.

The boy had been from the coast. Most likely a fisherman's son, looking to supplement the family income from a dwindling industry by signing up to serve in the Hermosian Army. He'd probably been fresh out of training.

It had been apparent to Kainan that the boy hadn't been fully prepared for what awaited him, and it had broken his heart. It had broken his heart to see the youngest of his country dying in the name of his foolish brother.

In that moment Kainan had blamed himself for the boy's death, because he'd known that when

Alek had begun to run amok he should have done more to rein in his brother. He'd tried. He'd tried hard. But then his brother had sought to end his life.

So Kainan had backed off and tried to help the people in another way. Serving as a surgeon on the front lines. But in moments like that, when that boy had lain there dying, afraid and alone, Kainan had questioned his choices.

And then Reagan had appeared, out of the darkness, in the quiet of the hospital where those on duty had been making their rounds on the patients who would live and trying to clean up the mess that the onslaught of injured soldiers from the front had caused.

She'd given the boy more medicine. More of the painkillers that had already been given to him. And then she'd sat next to him. Reagan could speak fluent Spanish, which was the mother tongue of Isla Hermosa, and she'd spoken to the boy.

Javier had been his name.

She'd held him. She cradled him in his arms and sung to him, just as she had sung to Andreas,

and Kainan had realized that she sang to many of those who were injured.

All he had been able to do was watch in awe as she'd administered the simplest form of healing: love, patience and human contact.

Reagan had held Javier as his tremors had ceased, as his breathing had become more shallow and as he'd breathed his last.

And she'd held him for a long time after. Singing to him…some sweet melody, something he had never heard before. But it hadn't mattered what she was singing. It had been her voice. It had been her kindness, her purity. So like his mother, who had helped the less fortunate, who had given everything to his father and got nothing in return.

It was in that moment that Kainan had melted for her. She might bottle up her emotions, but her compassion for others made her a brilliant, strong woman and he had desired her.

Only her.

He had seen her reaching out and comforting their son in the same way she had comforted Javier and all those other countless injured men and women from Isla Hermosa, Canada and the United States. It hadn't mattered to her what side

they'd fought for. She had afforded each and every single one of them the simple gift of human compassion and caring. To her there had been no borders, no colors and no religions. No conflict had been too great to stop her from delivering what they had all needed and that was love.

Reagan had cared for them all. She had judged no one.

And at that moment, seeing her being separated from their child, Kainan had realized that their son might never know what kind of strong woman his mother was and what a failure his father was.

It had broken his heart, and it had been too much for him to take in so he had turned away, missing that moment when they'd taken his son away.

He had turned back to find her trembling in front of the surgical wing, her eyes wide and her body looking as if it was about to bend and break under its burden. She'd been trying to stay strong, but her walls had come crashing down with the weight of it all. Of carrying the burden alone for too long.

That was why he'd picked her up and carried her away from it all. He hadn't cared who saw him in that moment. He'd wanted to afford her the same

amount of care and compassion she'd shown to everyone else. To make up for not being there when she'd needed him.

He wasn't sure he could *ever* make that up to her, but he'd try.

She'd helped so many and yet there had been no one helping her. He had seen that. She'd been alone and she'd been standing there so lost. So broken.

And he'd taken her in his arms, as she'd taken Javier in hers, and he'd held her. Comforted her. And then she'd kissed him.

He'd thought about her kisses ever since they'd parted. As he'd been transported on his way to Canada, with an endotracheal tube breathing for him, with no voice to cry out, he'd thought of her.

He'd longed for her.

When she'd kissed him he'd forgotten about being King. About the conflicts in Isla Hermosa. About his late brother and the damage he'd wrought.

All he'd cared about was the fact that he was in her arms again.

It had taken every ounce of his strength to step

back from her when she'd broken the kiss, because he'd burned for her. He still did.

And that was not proper.

It was selfish of him.

Perhaps he was just as selfish as his brother was?

No. You're nothing like him.

Still, he'd needed to put some distance between them, and yet now that it was morning he realized that, no matter how much distance there was between them, he would still feel the same.

His blunder of picking her up and carrying her to that boardroom, where he could hold her, had cost Reagan and Peter something. Their privacy.

Word had got out to the press about his behavior with Reagan. The world knew about her and Peter. Peter was no longer safe.

There were pictures of him carrying Reagan. And although he'd thought they were alone in that boardroom someone had managed to get a picture of them kissing.

He loathed being King in moments like this. Private, precious moments were made into entertainment for the rest of the world. Something cherished became tawdry and debased. It was no

longer a beautiful moment between Reagan and him. It belonged to the world.

He headed back to the pediatric critical care unit and watched Reagan sleeping. The guilt of subjecting her to this intrusion on her privacy was eating away at him.

I should've kept my distance from her in Isla Hermosa. I should've kept away.

He shouldn't have been so reckless, so selfish, but he could be *himself* around her. She gave him a sense of freedom that he'd never known. So he had been selfish, and had pursued her. When it came to Reagan he lost all sense.

Within a few hours the press and the rest of the world would know all about Reagan, and know that Kainan and Reagan had worked together in Isla Hermosa. He felt guilty that Reagan's life was going to be exposed. The press would chew her up and spit her out. They would twist everything about her.

He was going to try hard to protect her.

Reagan stirred and then sat up, seeing that he was standing by her.

"What time is it?" she asked groggily.

Seven in the morning, Kainan signed, and

handed her the coffee that he'd picked up in the hotel when he had been wandering. It was gourmet coffee, from his own country.

"Thank you." She took a sip. "Hermosian?"

He nodded. *You look like you didn't have a very comfortable sleep.*

"No, the chair was uncomfortable." She glanced back through the window. "But I'm used to cramming myself into hospital chairs and getting only a few hours of sleep while I'm waiting."

Was there anything to worry about last night?

"Nothing. Last time I talked to Sophie she said he was doing well." A wobbly smile spread across Reagan's face. "This will extend his life while we wait."

That's good.

Reagan stood and stretched. "I'm sorry, I'm a bit of a wreck. I can go change quickly, in the staff room, and then we can get to work."

No work today. I talked to Dr. McNeil. Christmas Eve is in two days and the medical students are already home for the holidays. I can work on my research and you can take some time to be with Peter.

"You spoke with Michael?"

Kainan held up his phone and grinned. *My robot voice did.*

Reagan laughed. "Well, if you need help with your research I can do it. I really don't want to be idle. I need to keep busy."

He didn't want to talk about his research, because it was no longer something he could focus on. Once he returned to Isla Hermosa he would no longer be a surgeon or be able to practice medicine. All his years of research would be left unfinished, and it was hard for him to think about, but it was a sacrifice he had to make.

He changed the subject. *Reagan, you do realize that in a couple of days, if Peter stays on this upward trajectory, he's going to come out of his medicated coma and he'll be able to come home.*

Reagan's eyes widened and she sat down slowly. "What?"

I thought you knew? Kainan signed.

"I *do* know." She shook her head. "It's just that he's never been home. Never. I had the nursery sort of complete…but it's not ready. My home is not ready."

Well, let's go check out your place and get it ready, then.

"You have your research to do."

It can wait. It had waited this long. *My security detail can take us there in the town car and I will help you.*

"You're abusing your power now, Your Majesty," she teased.

How? It's their duty to help the King's son. He grinned.

Reagan sighed. "I suppose so. I don't think I'm ready for this…"

Ready or not, you have to do this. There will be no need for him to be here while he waits for a heart. They will move him to the pediatric ward, out of this critical care unit, get us used to the portable ventricular assist device, and then we can take him home.

"We?"

Kainan smiled and then knelt down in front of her. *You know that I can protect you, Reagan. Please let me take care of you.*

"Kainan, I'm *not* accepting your proposal of marriage. Besides, you said that keeping us secret was the best form of protection that you could give us. If I…" She trailed off when she saw his expression. "The press know, don't they?"

Kainan nodded sadly. *When I carried you into the boardroom. There was someone from the press watching and they got a picture of us kissing.*

Reagan groaned. She set down her coffee cup on the floor beside the chair and rubbed her eyes. "This is horrible."

I'm sorry.

"It's not your fault."

It sort of is. I am King, after all.

And nothing about his life was his.

She laughed at that. "You're not helping."

Marry me. I can protect you.

"No. I can't. I can't think about that now, and I can't consider entering into that life with Peter still so fragile."

Kainan's stomach knotted. He'd known it was a long shot, but he'd had to keep trying. It was the only way to protect her and Peter, to provide for them. He had to do better than his father ever had.

Will you at least let me assist you with your apartment? he asked. *If you're with me I can protect you from the press.*

"Okay. Do you want to go now, while they still have Peter sedated?"

Kainan nodded. *I will go tell the team to get ready and you gather your things.*

"It's going to be a short visit to my apartment," she warned. "I want to be here when he wakes up. It's important that I'm here."

Of course.

Reagan picked up her coffee cup and left the pediatric critical care unit. Kainan sighed and looked back at his son, who still needed a machine to survive.

He knelt down, and even though he couldn't touch Peter he stared into his son's face. Emotion overcame him. This was his child. His flesh, his blood. He couldn't lose him.

"I will do better by you," he whispered. "I swear."

He bowed his head. He would be better than his father ever had.

Even if he wasn't there to show him.

She was trying not stare at Kainan, who was looking out of the window, his chin resting on his hand. She wanted to tell him that she'd seen him, that she'd heard what he'd said to their son.

Any kind of reservation had melted away when

she'd heard him whisper, "I will do better by you. I swear."

Reagan had had to leave the room or break down in front of him.

Kainan might be King, but he was good deep down. He was still that man she cared for.

He looked over and smiled. *Comfortable?*

"Very."

Reagan was thankful that Kainan had access to a town car, and that the car's windows were tinted, but the Hermosian flags that flew on the hood sort of gave them away.

"I thought you wanted to be the hidden King?" she said lightly.

Well, since word got out I thought it was time to use the embassy car that is kept here in Toronto. We can park anywhere. He grinned.

"That's good. There's not much parking near my place."

She didn't like it that they were in an embassy car, but if the world already knew about her then there was no sense in hiding. She could face whatever they threw at her. She was the one who'd got involved with Kainan.

Although it made her feel a bit nervous to be out with him.

How far away is your place?

"I don't know. It's fairly new. I got it when I first came back to Toronto and was preparing for Peter's arrival. I just know the distance in subway stops."

"What's the address?" the driver asked from the front seat. "There's GPS."

"Three-sixteen Richmond Street West. It's not that far, I guess. Like I said, I only know by subway stops and how many blocks I have to walk."

"You're right, Dr. Cote. It's not far. We'll be there and back in no time."

The driver plugged in the route map and Reagan turned back to Kainan.

"Thank you for helping me. I'm sure my place is a disaster. I really didn't have a lot of time to settle in. I was trying to work as long as I could at the hospital, to save up and have a decent maternity leave, and then… Well, you know the rest."

Peter was born and was so ill. Sadly, I do know the rest.

Kainan glanced out the window.

Perhaps he'll be on the regular pediatric floor

by Christmas? I hear they do a lot of celebrations for the children in there over Christmas and New Year's.

"Maybe he'll be home in time for New Year," said Reagan. And that thought was scary indeed.

A strange look passed over Kainan's face. *Yes. Perhaps.*

It didn't take the driver long to navigate the streets to her condo complex. He parked in front—legally, not having to resort to the embassy park-wherever-you-want privileges.

Kainan slid out first and then helped Reagan.

"No press here," she said, relieved.

I am glad of that. Especially since they know what you look like. I am sorry they were snapping your picture so much as we came out of the hospital. And you were bombarded with questions.

"I ignored them." She took out her key and opened the main door.

Before she called the elevator she opened up her mail slot and pulled out the copious amount of mail that had been piling since she'd last been there. One of the things on top was a Christmas card from her parents.

A knot formed in her stomach as she thought

about them. Thought how they didn't really care much for Peter—or her, for that matter. Still, what was socially acceptable was to send your offspring a Christmas card, and that was exactly what her mother had done. She was following protocol.

You haven't been back here in a while, I take it? Kainan signed, cocking an eyebrow as he glanced at her mail.

"No, I haven't."

What if you go into arrears on something?

"I do everything on my phone. There's an app for that," she teased.

She called the elevator and the doors opened up. She punched in her floor.

Her apartment was at the end of the hall. When she got to the door something seemed wrong. The door was splintered around the lock, and instead of having to put her key in she just turned the knob and it opened.

Kainan moved past her and into her apartment first. Reagan took a step inside and saw her place had been trashed.

The furniture was turned over and all her boxes had been opened up. Her things were everywhere, but her television and stereo were still there. Her

computer was as well, but it was plugged in, and when she touched it, it woke up. It was on, and it looked as if her system had been hacked. All her personal files…

She began to tremble. She hated it that this had happened. Her life was strewn across the floor in a shambles…exposed.

Kainan came from the bedroom.

This doesn't seem like a robbery for valuables. It looks like they were looking for information.

"Information about *me*?" she asked, in shock still.

Or your ties to me.

Kainan began to text.

"Who are you texting?"

"My security team" he said hoarsely.

He finished the text.

"I can't believe this has happened." She wanted to sit down, but if the police were going to come she didn't want to disturb any of the evidence. "Is your team calling the police?"

Kainan nodded. *I'm sorry this has happened, but I can protect you.*

Reagan snorted. "You've said that before, and look what's happened."

I'm sorry.

Reagan ignored him and set her mail down on her kitchen table. She made her way to her bedroom. The contents of her nightstand drawer had been dumped out on her bed, and her dresser had been rummaged through.

The few pieces of jewelry she had were still there. Kainan was right. They had been looking for information.

She went over to the walk-in closet and opened it to look at where she had started setting up a small nursery for Peter. Nothing had been touched.

Tears stung her eyes when she saw the crib that was waiting for him and the fine layer of dust on the wood. She was the worst mother ever. She hadn't even made it up. The sheet and quilt, even the hanging mobile, were still in a box.

All she had managed to do was set up the crib and a change table. There weren't even diapers in there yet.

"Big girls don't cry, Reagan. This was your choice!"

Reagan cursed under her breath. Angry at herself. Angry for letting her mother's words back in.

How was she going to bring home a baby on a

ventricular assist device and have him live here? This was no place for him. She was not ready for him to be out of the safe confines of the hospital. How was she going to be able to deal with this?

She picked up the small teddy bear that she'd bought for Peter three days before he was born. She held it close and tried not to cry again. She couldn't do this alone.

She didn't have to. Kainan had offered to help her. Kainan was *here*. But she wanted him to help her without having to make promises that she wasn't sure that she wanted to keep. She'd never wanted to get married. Not really.

Why couldn't they just work on raising Peter together?

Because Kainan will go back to Isla Hermosa after his surgery. He is King.

She had to do this on her own. Her parents were right in that she could only rely on herself. Peter was *her* responsibility. She had always been going to do this on her own anyway. Kainan's presence didn't change that. She had to protect her heart.

Kainan would do right by Peter, of that she was sure, but she wasn't so sure he would do the same for her, and she couldn't risk it.

He was King and he had a duty to his country. She understood that. She respected that.

Reagan set the bear back down. She would have to get used to doing things on her own. She couldn't leave Toronto. She had to stay close while they waited for Peter's new heart.

Kainan would return to Isla Hermosa to lead his country and Reagan would have to parent Peter on her own.

As she'd planned to do all along.

CHAPTER EIGHT

IT DIDN'T TAKE long for the police to arrive, and all Reagan could do was stand to the side and watch them go through her things, dusting for fingerprints and looking for evidence. She felt so exposed, so vulnerable, and she hated every minute of it.

"You say it doesn't appear that anything has been taken, Dr. Cote?" the constable in charge asked.

"Everything seems to be here—my computer, my television, and even some money that I had hidden in my sock drawer. Until I clean I won't really know."

The constable nodded.

Kainan signed and the constable glanced at her in question.

"He says he thinks that my personal information was stolen. It appears my computer was hacked into," she said.

"Why does the think that?" the constable asked.

"Because he's the King of Isla Hermosa and… we have a child together."

The constable was shocked. "This may have to be taken up with the RCMP."

"I understand," Reagan said stonily. "I know you'll do what's best."

Only right now she wasn't sure what that was.

The constable nodded. "We'll take your laptop in and have our forensic team go over it. There could be a digital trace."

"Thank you, Constable."

"No problem, Dr. Cote. Make sure you get your locks changed. As soon as we hear anything we'll give you a call."

The constable turned back to his team and they began to bag the evidence that they wanted to take a closer look at.

Reagan turned away. "What do you think they were after?" she asked Kainan.

They're were looking for information about you, me and our son. I have no doubts. Kainan shook his head. *I'm sorry this happened.*

"At least they didn't touch Peter's nursery. It's just as I left it."

Where is Peter's nursery? he asked.

"It's in the bedroom, in my walk-in closet."

Kainan frowned. *A closet?*

"It's a large closet, with a light. Lots of space. I was even able to fit a chair in there."

A closet seems highly inappropriate.

"Oh, yes? And what would you have me do? I'm alone and this is what I can afford."

His expression softened and she felt bad for snapping at him. It wasn't his fault that she'd thought he was dead.

You can't have a ventricular assist device in a walk-in closet.

"I'm aware of that now, but when I was pregnant I didn't think that my baby would be *on* a ventricular device."

Kainan sighed. "I'm sorry."

"It's okay. It's not your fault. I just feel..." She trailed off. *Violated. Afraid. Insecure.*

Only she didn't say those words out loud. She had been taught never to say things like that out loud. Never to show weakness.

"I'm tired."

Are you sure that's all? Kainan asked.

Reagan scrubbed a hand over her face. "I really

should get back to the hospital. We've been gone for ages. What if Peter wakes up?"

It will take a while before they wake him up. He has been sedated for so long. You won't miss it. Besides, you have to get these locks changed and we have to clean up this apartment.

Reagan nodded. "You're right. I'm just feeling a bit anxious right now."

And you have every right to be.

"We've got everything, Dr. Cote," the head constable said. "We'll keep you updated."

"Thank you, Constable. Have a merry Christmas."

"You too, Dr. Cote."

Reagan opened the door for the retreating police officers and shut it behind them. "I suppose I'd better call a locksmith to come and change the locks."

I'll start cleaning in the bedroom.

"I don't know where to start..." Reagan muttered.

One room at a time.

Kainan wandered away to her bedroom. She had no doubt that he was going to check out the

nursery she'd set up and tell her that it was unsuitable. And he wasn't wrong. It was unsuitable.

What am I going to do?

She felt lost at the moment. Everything was overwhelming her.

Step one: call the locksmith, and then you can think about step two.

Reagan looked up a local number on her phone and dialed, hoping someone would be able to come out on short notice right before Christmas.

Kainan wandered around the bedroom. It was small, but it was cozy. It was Reagan's room. Or it had been until a stranger had come in and violated her privacy.

Kainan clenched his fists, biting back the rage he was feeling thinking because someone had been in here. Someone who wanted information about him and Reagan.

This is all my fault.

If he hadn't got involved with Reagan this would never have happened.

He picked up a drawer that had been pulled out and tossed on the bed, slid it back into the dresser, remembering...

"Hey, can I get a picture of you?" the stranger had asked.

Kainan had looked up. "What?"

"You're a prince of Isla Hermosa, right?" There had been a blinding flash. "Come here."

"Who *are* you?" his mother had screamed as she'd thrown herself in front of him. "Get off my property!"

"Easy, Your Majesty. The public just wants pictures."

His mother had stood, her fists clenched. "Get off my property!"

The guards had soon been there, dragging the man away. When the photographer had been out of sight his mother had collapsed, trembling as she'd turned to him.

"He didn't hurt you, did he, Kainan?"

"No, Mama…"

He needed to protect Reagan, he thought now. And he couldn't protect her here.

He began to pluck clothing off the floor and fold the items, placing them back in the drawer. His gaze fell on the closed closet door. Kainan's pulse quickened as he thought about Peter. And,

though he knew he shouldn't look in the closet, he did.

He opened the closet door and flicked on the light.

Reagan had been right. It was a large closet, but it was a closet nonetheless, and his throat tightened when he saw the crib, the bedding in a bag on the floor, and the teddy bear that was lying on its side on a change table.

She had made it homey and cozy for their son. She had done the best she could, but it wasn't enough. Not for him.

He closed his eyes and guilt ate away at him for not being there. For not providing for them. She'd been all alone. This was not good enough for Reagan. She deserved more.

How? This will continue to happen. People will always pry into her life.

Even if Kainan didn't survive his surgery Peter was his heir and the press would be curious about him.

His throat tightened and it was hard to breathe. He closed his eyes and tried not to think of the moment when he'd tried to speak and hadn't been able to. When he hadn't been able to breathe.

"Kainan?" Reagan called out, and then she appeared in the doorway of the room.

Kainan set the bear back down, sitting him upright, and stepped out of the closet, closing the door behind him.

"Checking up on my handiwork?" she asked.

He smiled. *Perhaps.*

"The locksmith is here and I've cleaned up the living room the best I can. Once the lock is changed and I've grabbed a few things I want to get back to the hospital."

Of course. And I will have Andreas pack up the baby's things.

"What're you talking about?" she asked.

You can't stay here. It's not safe.

"Kainan, this is my *home*. This will be Peter's home. Where else would we go?"

I will get you a new place. One that is more suitable.

"I don't think so."

I do think so, Kainan signed. *Peter needs a larger room and you need to be moved somewhere safe. My security team will handle it.*

"No, I'm not uprooting my life, Kainan. That's too much to ask."

You won't marry me, and you won't let me protect you. Let me do this. I can't have you come back here and be pestered. Not when Peter needs to rest and heal.

Reagan bit her lip. She was clearly thinking about it, but she didn't answer.

It will be days before he's discharged, Kainan signed. *More than enough time to get you a new place, close to the hospital, and move you. You won't have to do anything. Let me do this, Reagan. Please.*

"Fine," she said. "But it has to be close to the hospital."

I will find something.

He was relieved he could do something for them. That he could take care of them this way.

Kainan texted his team to let them know what he required. The new place would be large enough to house Reagan and Peter, and Kainan would be in a suite next to him, with his security detail.

Though Reagan didn't need to know that bit of information yet.

The press knew that he was at the Royal York and were camped out there permanently, so moving to a new location with a secure entrance would

be better. He would be closer to Peter and Reagan and maybe, just maybe, he would be able to convince Reagan to marry him. Then he could keep them safe behind the palace walls.

Really?

That was his father's thinking, and he hated himself for it, but he felt powerless and didn't know what to do.

He was broken.

But he wasn't going to let Reagan or Peter out of his sight.

Kainan dropped Reagan at the hospital, where she wanted to be, and then went with Andreas to see a new place.

The condo was located two blocks south of the hospital and on the lakeshore. It had two suites, side by side, and one of them would comfortably house his security staff and himself. The smaller suite was larger than Reagan's current home, and would be more than adequate for her and Peter.

The only downside was that it wasn't on the subway route, but it was only a block to Union Station and the hospital was right across the street from that.

Reagan could walk or Andreas could drive her. If he was still here. If Kainan's voice surgery was successful then Andreas would return to Isla Hermosa with him.

But you can come back.

He wasn't sure about that. Would Reagan forgive him if he left?

He wasn't sure.

"They're just waiting for your signature, Your Majesty. I have made sure that they have signed confidentiality agreements and I have paid in cash," Andreas said, interrupting his thoughts.

Thank you, Andreas. How soon can we move in?

"Today," Andreas said. "I can have movers go to Dr. Cote's apartment and pack it up, so we can get her into this new home by tomorrow morning."

Do that.

Andreas nodded and opened the door to the condo complex. Kainan went through all the paperwork and signed everything that was needed.

Tonight he would tell Reagan about the plan over dinner. Even if he had to bring it into the hospital again. He wasn't giving her a chance to say no this time. This was for their own protection. This was something he could do for them.

They would be in their new home in time for Christmas, and perhaps this way he could show Reagan he was in. That if he left he would still be there.

How can you be "in" as King?

And then there was his surgery coming up. With the amount of scar tissue in his throat it was risky. He might die, abandoning Reagan.

He shook that thought away as he took the keys from the realtor and followed Andreas to the top floor of the complex.

"The suites are at the end of the hallway," Andreas said as he led Kainan down. "Dr. Cote's is twenty-nine B and you're twenty-nine A."

Kainan nodded and turned the key to Reagan's new place. It was bright and large. There were windows which faced the icy grey waters of Lake Ontario. He could not see the CN Tower from this viewpoint, but that was okay. The view of the islands and the water was all he needed.

It reminded him of Isla Hermosa. Endless water and islands scattered all around the main island. The only difference was that Isla Hermosa was tropical and here there was snow. And the grey, ice-filled water was a bit unforgiving.

Kainan was not a fan of winter.

Still, this was a much better space than her current home. She was surrounded by tall buildings there. It was stifling, as if there was no room to breathe. Here at the top of this complex, with Lake Ontario stretching below him, he felt he could breathe.

"Do you like it, Your Majesty?" Andreas asked.

Kainan nodded. and then handed Andreas the key that Reagan had given him when the locksmith had changed her locks.

Please make sure that Reagan is moved in right away.

"And what of you, Your Majesty?"

Get some furnishings. My room can be packed up later. I want us to have a close-by option—especially since we don't know how long Peter will still be in the hospital.

Andreas nodded. "Very well, Your Majesty."

Thank you for all your assistance, Andreas. I don't think I express it enough.

Andreas was a bit taken aback by that. "Thank you, Your Majesty."

There was a buzz on Kainan's phone and he

looked down to see that it was Reagan texting him. There was news about Peter.

I have to go back to the hospital. Kainan slipped his phone in his pocket.

"I will take you back there right now."

Kainan followed Andreas out of the apartment. He was glad things were moving forward with Reagan, because he was running out of time.

Reagan's pulse was racing. They had just moved Peter from the pediatric critical care unit to the regular pediatric ward. He was doing so well on the ventricular assist device that they were going to bring him out of sedation.

She would be able to hold him. She hadn't held him in so long. Her arms were aching to hold him, but she was terrified too.

Deep down she was scared of this whole thing. It was a way to extend his life, but there was a set time-frame. Peter needed a new heart. There was no other choice.

There was a new set of nurses on duty and she waited with bated breath as they moved about the room. Peter was moving, and there were more subtle movements as the sedation wore off.

She'd done a rotation on Pediatrics when she had

been an intern, but she had forgotten how resilient kids were. How they bounced back.

She'd texted Kainan to come, because he'd wanted to know when they were going to wake Peter up.

She knew he was out property-hunting, but she seriously doubted that he would find anything on short notice. And, even though he didn't want her going back to her apartment alone, she was going to head back there and get Peter's nursery ready.

Kainan came into the room.

"Glad you could make it," she said, and she *was* relieved that he was here.

How is he doing? Kainan signed.

"Good. He's strong."

Kainan nodded and picked up the chart to read the notes. A brief smile crossed his face as he shut the chart.

This is good!

"I'll be back in a few minutes, Reagan," the pediatric nurse said. "I have to check on my other patients."

"Thanks, Maria," Reagan said.

Maria nodded and left the room.

Reagan took a step forward and stared down at her baby, wrapped up in his crib. There was a

cannula running from his chest to the machine that sat on the table next to the crib. The machine that was pumping blood instead of his heart now.

His poor, weak heart.

She reached out to touch him but then took her hand back because she wasn't wearing gloves. She looked up at Kainan, unsure.

What's wrong? he signed.

"I'm not wearing gloves—just a surgical gown."

Did they tell you that you needed to be gowned and gloved?

"No, they didn't. I just put this on out of habit."

Kainan smiled gently at her. *Go ahead.*

Reagan reached out and touched Peter's smooth, soft skin. Emotion overcame her as she ran her fingers over his tiny hand and then over the dark curls on his head.

"I've waited so long for this," she whispered.

The tears were threatening to spill, but she cleared her throat—because this wasn't the end of scares. This was just a way to keep him alive longer, until a heart became available.

She couldn't let her guard down yet.

Peter stirred under her hand and she gasped. His head moved and he opened his eyes, blink-

ing. And then those dark eyes that were so like Kainan's looked toward her. His brow furrowed as he tried to make sense of what he could seen through a drug-induced fog.

"Peter..." she whispered, she knelt down to look at his little chubby face. "Mommy's here."

Her voice hitched in her throat and it took every ounce of her strength not to cry as she connected with her son in his crib.

Peter's eyes closed, but he smiled. So many stages of his life she'd missed. Babies grew so fast and she was missing it.

There will be more stages that you will get to see, she told herself.

And for the first time in a long time she confidently believed that.

Then Kainan knelt down and stared at his son, his eyes glistening, and he beamed as Peter opened his eyes again and looked at Kainan.

"He has my eyes," Kainan said, and Reagan could see the pride in his face.

"Did he open his eyes?" Maria asked as she returned.

"He did," Reagan said, standing up.

"That's wonderful. It will take a while for him

to fully wake out of his sedation, but he's doing very well," Maria said.

"How long do you think it will be before he's discharged?" Reagan asked, nervous about the answer, because here in the hospital he was safe.

"It's hard to say. It depends how well he does and his pain management. But since you're both surgeons Dr. McNeil will probably discharge him as early as Christmas Eve. And that will be an excellent Christmas gift!" Maria continued, checking Peter's lines as Reagan stood there in shock.

"That soon?" Reagan murmured in disbelief. "I have a lot to do to get ready."

Maria grinned. "I'm sure. Why don't you go do that, Dr. Cote? He will likely be asleep for a while longer. Get some diapers and get his nursery ready."

Reagan was about to argue when Michael entered Peter's room. He looked a bit panicked.

"Reagan, I'm so glad I found you," Michael said breathlessly, and then he saw Kainan. "Dr. Laskaris, I'm glad you're here too."

Dread crept down her spine. "What's wrong, Michael?"

"A section of the roof has collapsed at the shop-

ping center. A lot of people are injured and I'm short-staffed due to the snowstorm that just rolled in off the lake. It's dumped three inches of snow since it started two and half hours ago."

"What?"

Reagan opened the blinds in Peter's room and couldn't even see the courtyard of the hospital. Just a wall of white.

"They're bringing them in on foot and our emergency room is packed," Michael said. "I could use you both."

Kainan signed, and she knew what he was thinking.

"Kainan wants to know how he can help even when he can't communicate," Reagan said.

"He can work with you, Reagan. I'm sorry to pull you away from your son, but it's all hands on deck."

Kainan nodded with determination and picked up his jacket.

"We'll be right there, Michael," Reagan said.

Michael left at a sprint.

"Don't worry, Dr. Cote. Peter will be fine," Maria said.

Reagan nodded, but she was unsure about leav-

ing him. Still, she was needed. She was a surgeon and there were lives to be saved.

Kainan held open the door for her and they walked together to the staff change room, where all the on-call doctors who'd been able to get in were getting ready for the onslaught of patients.

There was also a team of doctors who would be working on clearing the operating theaters of non-essential surgeries and keeping the flow to X-Ray and the CT scanner free and clear. As well as finding bed space in an already cramped hospital.

Reagan changed quickly, stuffing her clothing into her locker. Kainan stood beside her, unbuttoning the dress shirt that he'd been wearing.

"No locker," he said quickly as he stuffed his clothes into hers.

"Save your voice, Kainan," she said as she shimmied out of her dress pants and pulled on her scrubs. "You're going to need it."

He smiled sadly and nodded as he grabbed a pair of men's scrubs from the shelf behind him.

She thought about all those times in the tight quarters of the field hospital and how much carnage they had seen and worked together on.

This was going to be the same.

A section of the roof falling in a packed shop-

ping center at Christmas… The thought made her sick to her stomach.

After they were dressed and ready to go, with disposable surgical gowns and gloves, they headed straight into the chaos of the emergency room.

Michael was in charge as he spoke to his surgeons and assigned stations, putting the residents outside to receive the patients as they came in from the ambulances.

Kainan went straight to work and began to set up other triage areas for the less critical. Reagan translated for him and helped him to divide a hallway that was rarely used into small pods for the less injured.

The waiting room was packed as well, with patients who had wandered in with things like colds, sprains and an assortment of other cases. They would have to be seen to. and Michael mobilized a group of residents to take care of them and prioritize.

Reagan and Kainan worked well together, just as they had always done. She knew what he was thinking before he had to ask her, and vice versa.

"Just like old times, eh?" she teased.

Kainan made a funny face. Before he could respond there was the wail of sirens. Ambulances

were working their way through the snow. Orderlies were outside, working on shoveling a clear path as the first ambulance pulled up.

"Reagan and Kainan—you're up!" Michael called over the commotion.

Reagan went outside, the bitter cold biting at her cheeks as the ambulance came to a stop. The doors opened and the paramedics jumped into action.

"Male, age forty-five, multiple injuries to the torso and abdomen. Glasgow coma scale of two on arrival."

Reagan and Kainan helped the paramedic push the gurney through the snow and they took their patient to one of the trauma bays that were being used for priority patients. A man with multiple crush injuries to the torso and abdomen and a GCS of two was a priority.

Kainan signed off on the paramedics' charts while Reagan began to go over the man's ABCs. One pupil was blown. and she was worried that when he fell he'd hit his head hard and there might be a hematoma.

Kainan worked on the other side of her. He snapped his fingers to get her attention and

signed, *Free fluid in the lungs. I'm going to do a chest tube.*

Reagan nodded. "Left pupil is blown. I want to get him down for a CT."

"Chest tray," Kainan said gruffly to the intern who was in the room with them, and he rolled his shoulders, wincing from the pain of exerting his voice. But he didn't hesitate as he cut away the man's shirt and examined his chest.

"Any lacerations from the debris that landed on him? I see blood," Reagan said as she started a large-bore IV and hung painkillers and fluids.

Kainan held up two fingers.

Reagan counted at least four wounds to the man's abdomen. There was also dark bruising under his skin. "He needs a CT scan as soon as you get that chest tube in."

She cursed inwardly as she tried to picture how the debris had fallen on the patient and what organs it might have damaged. Because there was fluid in the man's lungs she had no doubt that he was suffering a hemothorax, but what other damage had the debris caused?

"Here you are, Dr. Laskaris," the intern said, handing the chest tube tray to Kainan.

Kainan nodded and went about listening and finding the best place to insert the chest tube. He quickly wiped the skin and then made his move.

The patient flexed in a decerebrate motion, arching his chest and his head, arms straight out, everything stiff in response to the chest tube being inserted.

As it did its job the patient's vitals steadied. Kainan smiled and secured the tube and they readied the patient to go down for the CT scan. Reagan needed to see what she was dealing with before she went in there and tried to fix the damage that had been done.

Kainan moved beside her silently, anticipating her every move. Just like in Isla Hermosa.

They were as one.

And, though she'd always prided herself on being a lone wolf, she was glad he was here in this moment. That he was here with her now and that she didn't have to explain her every move. He just *knew*.

And that thought scared her.

It scared her to think that she needed him when she had never needed anyone before.

CHAPTER NINE

"CAN YOU MOVE the retractor, please?" Reagan asked, and Kainan adjusted his hold on it.

Their patient had some head trauma, but nothing as serious as what was going on in his abdomen, because there were crush injuries and he was bleeding internally. The CT scan had shown her what damage had been done.

The spleen had been lacerated and was bleeding heavily. A kidney had been pierced, as well as his bowel, and the diaphragm, which was why his lungs had filled with blood. The heart was fine for now, as was the liver. Still, the bleeding needed to be controlled so he didn't die before they had a chance to repair his injuries.

She was hours into surgery. They were still hanging blood, but she was getting ahead of the damage. Even though Kainan could not speak he knew what to do, and she didn't often have to ask

for his assistance. It was if he knew what her next step would be before she did.

They worked so well together. She'd forgotten how much she enjoyed working with him. Working with him to save lives.

The King of Isla Hermosa.

She shook her head, trying not to think about that fact. He was a surgeon too. He hadn't been a king when they'd worked together, when he'd taken her in his arms.

He had just been Kainan.

Now he was King, and yet here he was helping save lives. How many world leaders would do the same? It was at this moment that she saw the man he'd been before—the man she'd known and cared for.

She watched him briefly as a resident worked on stitching, studying him over her surgical mask. Those kind eyes were looking down at the work the resident was doing with keen interest, and she couldn't help but smile as she thought of him by her side, working with her as if nothing had changed.

It was nice, even though the situation was not. And her pulse quickened as she thought back to

that kiss they'd shared, when Peter was in surgery for the ventricular device. His strong arms had comforted her, as had his kiss, and their connection had grounded her.

Kainan was her rock.

The realization shocked her, and she wasn't sure how she felt about it. She had been taught not to rely on anyone. So when had she begun to rely on Kainan so much?

It made her stomach twist in a knot, because she *had* to be self-sufficient. She couldn't rely on him, no matter how much she wanted to.

He was King of a foreign country and would eventually have to return to it. She couldn't leave Canada—not until Peter had a new heart. She had to be careful not to let *her* heart do all her thinking, which was what was happening when she was around Kainan.

She had to start thinking logically. She had to be careful. Peter's heart wasn't the only one that was fragile—hers was too.

They had been working on this man for hours, but he was going to make it and that was the most important thing. After they'd finished up here they would have to scrub out and head back down

to the emergency room and continue to work, to take the pressure off a bombarded trauma room.

On a tray across the operating room she could see her phone sitting there, silent, as a nurse monitored it.

Peter's fine. And after this is all done you can hold him.

Just that simple thought sustained her. It kept her focused.

She finished the surgery and gave instructions to the scrub nurse and the intern for the patient's postoperative care. Kainan followed her out of the operating room and they scrubbed out.

"Where to?" Kainan asked, and then winced, his throat paining him.

"Have you had your throat looked at by your otolaryngologist lately?"

Kainan sent her an exasperated expression. *Of course.*

"It's just that I know if you use your voice more than you should it can cause problems. I would hate for you to risk your surgery."

It's already a risky surgery and there is a lot of scar tissue.

"Why have they waited so long?"

The surgeon wanted to wait until I was strong.

"And…?" Reagan asked, drying off her hands. "You're stronger now."

Kainan pursed his lips together. *The surgery is coming, but there's no guarantee it will work.*

"I think it will," she said.

Why do you think so?

"A king needs a voice," she said.

I have you.

It was like a punch in her gut. "I won't always be there to be your voice, Kainan."

Why not? You could be my Queen. It's a solution that would work for us both. We'd give Peter stability and you could assist me in my rule.

"I'm a surgeon, Kainan. Could I still practice medicine as Queen of Isla Hermosa?"

Kainan's shoulders slumped and she had her answer. She felt bad for Kainan, because soon his surgical career would be over. He was a king, and when he returned to Isla Hermosa he wouldn't be able to practice medicine any longer.

"You need to stop proposing to me, Kainan. You know my answer. It's no."

But the more time she spent with him the harder it was to say no. The dream of a happy family

she'd always craved was tempting, but nothing worked out the way it was supposed to and she didn't want to risk it.

He didn't say anything, and didn't look her in the eye. It was hard to disappoint him, but she couldn't let her heart make this decision.

If her heart had had its way then she would have said yes the first time he'd asked her. The moment he'd walked back in her life.

You're a fool, her heart told her, but she knew that it would never work. The only person she could rely on was herself.

They headed back down to the emergency room and it was still chaotic. As she surveyed the scene her gaze landed on a tall man with dark hair in one of the beds. Alone and clearly in pain.

"Isn't that Andreas?" she asked.

Kainan spun around, pained as he rushed to his security guard's side with Reagan at his heels. He had been hurt, but it looked like just a flesh wound.

"Andreas," Reagan said sadly. "You were at the shopping center?"

"Dr. Cote..." He grimaced, and then his gaze fell on Kainan. "Your Majesty. I'm sorry."

For what? Kainan signed.

Andreas leaned back against the pillows, his face with the grey tint of pain and blood loss.

Reagan pulled his chart. "Your leg was caught under a cement beam, but it's not broken, and the laceration missed your femoral artery. That's good."

Andreas nodded. "It's just a flesh wound. I was trying to protect a child from the falling debris."

Kainan winced and bowed his head, gripping Andreas's shoulder.

"You have lost a lot of blood," she said, then bit her lip and stopped the resident who was dealing with Andreas. "Has blood been ordered? His platelet count is low."

"Yes, but the blood bank doesn't have any universal blood. There's another blood bank across the city, and they're trying to get through with the type of blood he needs, but the storm and this accident has depleted our reserves," the resident said.

Dammit.

I will donate blood, Kainan signed. *I'm Hermosian and I can donate for him.*

The resident looked confused.

"He can donate," Reagan said. "He's a universal blood type and both of them are Hermosian. Ready a transfusion kit and get this man on plasma while I handle the donation."

"Yes, Dr. Cote." The resident ran away.

"We'll be back, Andreas. Do you need anything for the pain?" Reagan asked.

Andreas shook his head. "No, Dr. Cote. I am fine. The child I helped lives, and that's the main thing, but I cannot accept blood from my King."

Reagan frowned and Kainan's brow furrowed.

You will, Kainan said.

"Your Majesty, I can't take your blood."

It's just blood, Kainan signed furiously. *You will take it and that is a royal decree.*

Andreas sighed and closed his eyes. "Yes, Your Majesty."

Kainan pulled the drapes around Andreas's bed. His face was like thunder. Andreas's injury was obviously bothering him. It bothered Reagan too. She hated to see Andreas hurt again. When he'd been injured during the Hermosian uprising it had been because he'd pulled a younger soldier out of the line of fire.

It seemed bizarre that on the front lines of bat-

tle in a foreign country they had more blood than here in a vast city, and all because of a snowstorm which was hampering their ability to get to it. It was silly.

Kainan took a seat in an exam room just outside the emergency department. He pulled off his white lab coat and stuck out his arm.

The resident brought Reagan the kit she would need to get the blood donation from Kainan. Reagan began to ready everything while Kainan stared at the wall, still fuming.

"Are you all right?"

Kainan nodded, but he wouldn't look at her.

"What's wrong? Are you mad at Andreas?"

No, he signed. *I'm angry at myself.*

"Why? You had nothing to do with his injury."

I sent him out to furnish my new apartment.

She raised her eyebrows as she wiped his arm with rubbing alcohol. "*Your* new apartment. I thought you were looking for a place for me and Peter?"

We found that too. They're next to each other.

She raised an eyebrow. "How convenient."

A small smile tugged at his lips. *Peter is my*

son too, and I want to be close to him for as long as I can.

Right, because he would have to leave. There was an expiry date on his time in Canada.

"Sorry, of course you do." Then she realized what he was saying. "You got apartments that are available now?"

Kainan nodded. *With the right amount of money.*

"Kainan, how *much* money?" She'd agreed to a new place, but she didn't want him spending great sums of money on her.

There is no mortgage to worry about, Reagan. You can raise Peter there comfortably. And when I'm in Toronto I can be close to him.

Reagan cursed under her breath. "You shouldn't have done that."

He's my son too. I just want him to be comfortable. And I want to take care of you.

"Kainan, I have to be self-sufficient. I *can't* rely on you. When you leave it will just be me and Peter."

Kainan didn't respond. He set his jaw firmly in that stubborn way of his and looked away from her.

"So, when are the movers coming for my stuff—

or have you arranged that too?" she asked sarcastically.

He grinned and she groaned.

"I'm probably already moved in, aren't I?"

In the process.

She shook her head and then tied the tourniquet around his arm. "Make a fist—and no more signing."

Kainan rolled his eyes, but that smug grin was still on his face.

She got the blood transfusion started and then removed the tourniquet. Kainan was a pro at this.

"It's not your fault for sending him to that shopping center, Kainan. A roof collapsed. No one is at fault. Things happen."

Kainan didn't say anything. He just closed his eyes and looked at the ceiling. She couldn't blame him. One of the things that bothered her about medicine was blood donation. It was good to do it, but she'd got a bit queasy the couple of times she had donated over the years.

"What you're doing for Andreas is good," she said. "You're a good king to your people. You may think you need a voice, but you don't. Your actions speak louder than your words ever will."

He raised his head and looked at her then, those dark eyes twinkling, and he mouthed the words *thank you* before closing his eyes and staring back up at the ceiling.

Kainan stood and watched as Andreas received his blood transfusion. After he'd donated he'd felt a bit dizzy, and Reagan had got him some orange juice and let him rest before she'd been called away by a resident.

When Kainan had felt better he'd headed back to the emergency room and gone to check on Andreas, who had already been hooked up to an intravenous and receiving Kainan's donation.

The color was returning to his friend's cheeks now.

Kainan still felt incredible guilty that Andreas had been put in harm's way. Twice.

He didn't like putting people's lives at risk. He was a surgeon. He *saved* lives.

You're no longer a surgeon, though.

And that thought sobered him. He was King, and a country full of lives depended on him. His life was no longer his.

Still, there was a part of him that didn't want to

be King. Being back in the operating room and working with Reagan had been amazing. He'd forgotten what it was like to save a life. He hadn't practiced surgery since the day Reagan had left Isla Hermosa.

He missed it.

Missed the thrill of it all.

Still, if he died on the operating table with a surgeon trying to save his voice then there would be no monarchy for Isla Hermosa. Peter was too young to be King and he was the last of his line.

Unless you appoint a regent to take Peter's place. An illegitimate king can still rule when he comes of age, as long as he's claimed, in writing, by the current King.

Reagan came in and glanced at Kainan in the seat next to Andreas's bedside. Andreas was still sleeping.

"You okay?" she asked.

Tired, but I will live.

"So will Andreas. Don't worry—your blood helped."

I know. Even if he didn't want it.

"I don't get that."

Because I'm King and...

"And?" she asked.

"It's not right," Andreas repeated, still in delirium.

Kainan chuckled softly as he looked at Andreas. *He's my half brother.*

Reagan's eyes widened. "Your half brother?"

Yes, though not legitimate. Andreas thinks of his adoptive father as his real father, not the late King. His adoptive father claimed him as his own, which is why Andreas could never be in the line of succession. He was luckier than me.

"Luckier? Why?"

He was loved and doted on. He had freedom. I did not. Kainan scrubbed a hand over his face. *I envied him for so many years.*

"Do you still?"

He looked up at her. If he'd had Andreas's life he probably wouldn't be a surgeon, and he wouldn't have met Reagan. For the first time he didn't envy Andreas's different upbringing.

No.

Pink bloomed in her cheeks. She cleared her throat. "How is your voice?"

He spoke aloud. "My throat is tight…sore. I

should go see Dr. Shaw. Can you keep an eye on Andreas?"

She nodded, her gaze soft. "Yes."

Andreas opened his eyes. "Your Majesty?"

Kainan stood up and squeezed Andreas's shoulder. *Rest*, he signed.

Kainan left Andreas to sleep. He made his way out of the emergency room and to Dr. Shaw's office. Dr. Shaw had been the surgeon who'd looked at his throat when he'd first arrived in Toronto, and he had the information from the Ottawa surgeon about the surgical procedures that Kainan had endured in the field.

Dr. Shaw was packing up for the evening when Kainan knocked on his door. Dr. Shaw also knew American Sign Language, because of all the hearing-impaired patients he worked with. Which was fortuitous.

"Dr. Laskaris—or should I refer to you as Your Majesty?"

Kainan smiled. *Kainan will suffice.*

"It's some crazy storm out there, eh? I think I'm going to leave my car in the employee garage and take the subway home—although the tracks at Rosehill are covered."

I'm worried about scar tissue. I've been using my voice, Kainan signed.

Dr. Shaw's eyebrows rose. "Have you? How much? I told you not to overdo it."

Kainan ignored that. This was his chance to be strong for his son, for Reagan. He needed his voice.

Could you please check?

"I can." Dr. Shaw set his bag down and took a seat, firing up his computer as Kainan shut the door. "Hopefully you haven't overtaxed yourself too much."

I hope not. I need my voice by the New Year.

Dr. Shaw nodded and examined his throat, frowning. "The surgery may not work. Although during your last scan there were not as many adhesions. I would like to get another scan, but I can still do your surgery on December twenty-sixth."

Kainan nodded. *Of course. When would you like the scan done?*

"Tomorrow morning, if that's okay? I know your boy just had surgery…"

Tomorrow is fine. My son is stable and I need to get this taken care of.

Dr. Shaw nodded. "Dr. McNeil told me that

when you asked for the surgery I was to make it happen as if you were a head of state."

I appreciate it, and I'm sorry for inconveniencing you, but I was told you were the best.

"You're not inconveniencing me, Kainan." Dr. Shaw stood and Kainan did as well. "It's my pleasure. Come by my office tomorrow at seven in the morning and we'll get you down to the MRI and get it done. We'll see what we're working with. And stop using your voice!"

I will.

"I'm serious—no more talking. No more exercising it. I will see you tomorrow, Kainan."

Kainan shook Dr. Shaw's hand before heading back to the emergency room. He texted Andreas's second in command to see how the move was going and to let them know what had happened to Andreas.

He had to step up and do what was right.

He was terrified that he wouldn't survive surgery, which meant he would lose Reagan forever, leaving her and Peter alone.

Never know his son.

Never have happiness.

CHAPTER TEN

REAGAN HAD BEEN separated from Kainan since just after he'd donated blood for Andreas. She'd got pulled into another surgery. An injured person had been brought in and could only communicate in Spanish.

She'd planned to take Kainan into surgery with her, but then she had been informed that this man was a Hermosian refugee and, given Andreas's reaction to Kainan donating blood, she'd thought it was best to keep the King out of the operating room.

Her patient was sedated, so Reagan went about repairing the injuries that he had sustained when the roof had collapsed on top of him.

Thankfully, no one had died in the accident.

Not even her first patient, Mr. Lucas, with the multiple crush injuries and the head injury. Reagan had saved his life.

When she came out of surgery the chaos in the emergency room had died down, as had the snow.

It was after midnight, which meant that it was Christmas Eve now. Officially.

She was exhausted, but she had to find Kainan.

When she went down to the emergency room, where the staff were now cycling through the non-emergent cases that had come in, she saw that Andreas was being moved to a room for overnight observation.

"Dr. Cote," Andreas said, smiling.

"How are you feeling?" she asked.

"Better. I would like to leave, but they want to keep me."

"You just had a major laceration and a blood transfusion. You need to rest here. Have you seen Kainan? I'm afraid I had to go into surgery and I lost track of him."

"Yes, I saw him a few hours ago. He was going to speak to another doctor before he checked on Peter, and then I believe he was headed back to the hotel to pack up his things because his new residence will be ready soon."

"I heard about that," Reagan said, crossing her arms.

Andreas grinned. "He will have the key to your

new place, and I know that my team has got everything in your old place moved out. Do you want me to put your old place on the market?"

"I can handle that, Andreas. You need your rest."

"If you want to speak to Kainan you'll need this," Andreas reached in his pocket and pulled out a gold elevator keycard. "It's my extra copy and it will allow you to access his room."

"Thanks. I think I will go see him after I check on Peter."

Andreas nodded and the orderly wheeled him away.

Reagan turned the keycard over in her hand. She really needed to talk to Kainan, especially since they were planning on discharging Peter soon. They had to talk about the arrangements and what would happen when Kainan returned to Isla Hermosa.

How much longer could he stay here? He had duties to do.

Reagan pocketed the card and went to the staff change room. She got out of her scrubs and put them in the laundry hamper, changing back into her street clothes.

She went to check on Peter and found he was still asleep, but he stirred when she touched him gently. Things were looking up. Even though Peter relied on a machine to keep him alive, he was here and responding. He was no longer in a medicated coma.

Even if Kainan left she would have Peter.

Except Peter wouldn't have Kainan.

That made her sad, but the timing was off. Kainan was King and his country needed him, and Peter needed a new heart. He had to stay in Toronto while he waited.

Reagan kissed her son's head and then left the hotel. She needed to have something to eat and a nap, and Kainan was the one who had the key to her new place where supposedly her bed and all her belongings were.

She didn't even know the address!

Reagan slipped down through the abandoned PATH walkway, which was devoid of commuters now, with the underground shops closed for the night. Then she went up the spiral staircase that connected The Royal York to the underground.

She was heading toward the gold elevators when she saw that Kainan was hanging out in a deserted

piano lounge. He was playing the grand piano. The music was sad and haunting.

She headed toward him. Such strong hands, but gentle in the way he handled patients...and her. He was an imposing king, but he was so kind and sweet with their son.

It had completely knocked down her barriers to see him with Peter.

All her fears about Kainan being distant and not caring about Peter had evaporated away.

Kainan *cared*.

And she was lost to him. She was weak when it came to him and in this moment she didn't care.

Kainan glanced up as she approached him and smiled halfheartedly, scooting over so she could sit next to him.

"I didn't know you played," she said.

He didn't respond, but finished his piece and then turned to her.

I don't play often, but it helps clear my head. Where were you?

"I got pulled into surgery on another injured patient. He was a Hermosian refugee."

Kainan grimaced. "A Hermosian refugee?"

"Yes," she said carefully.

"Did he live?"

"Yes."

"That's good." Kainan rubbed his eyes. "I feel responsible for him—for all my people. As King, I feel it was my duty to keep my country together. My people shouldn't be here as refugees."

"It wasn't your fault that war broke out in your country. You weren't King then."

"I know, but I'm King *now* and it's my responsibility."

"He's safe here in Canada. As are you."

Kainan nodded, but didn't smile. He was sad, and it was apparent that the burden of his people weighed heavily on him.

That's good.

"I came to ask you where I live now," she said with a small smile.

Yes, I suppose that's important. Kainan reached into his pocket and pulled out a key. He handed it to her. *Your new condo is Golden Centre condos on Queens Quay. Your apartment twenty-nine B.*

"Thanks." Reagan pocketed the key. "They're going to send Peter home later today, and it's Christmas Eve."

Kainan nodded. *I know. It will be good. What should we do?*

"I need to go to my new place and make sure that Peter's room is ready." She was puzzled. "What do you mean, what should *we* do?"

To celebrate?

"I don't know." She laughed. "I never thought that I'd have anything to celebrate. I think I just need to ready Peter's room and make a home for him. I think that's all I can handle now."

Would you like to go there now? We can take a cab. Most of my security detail is over at my new place anyway.

"They left you alone here?"

They don't know that I'm here, actually. They think that I'm still at the hospital.

"I suspect that they wouldn't be too happy to learn that you were here."

Kainan shrugged. *Do you want to go?*

"Yes. I wouldn't mind having a short nap in my own bed for a change."

Kainan nodded. *That can be arranged. Let's go, then, it's late.*

They walked out of the empty piano lounge and headed out onto Front Street. The snow had

stopped falling and the streets had been freshly plowed. Even though it was long after midnight there were still taxis waiting outside the prestigious hotel.

Kainan opened the door and Reagan slid in, telling the cabdriver the address. It didn't take the cabdriver long, on the deserted streets of Toronto, to get to the new condo building.

Reagan's mouth hung open when she saw it. She knew exactly how much these suites were. When she'd first moved back to Toronto, just pregnant, this building had been half-complete. She'd looked at purchasing a suite, but hadn't been able to swing it.

It was the perfect location. Even better than her apartment on Richmond Street West.

Do you like it? Kainan signed.

"It's too much," she whispered.

She paid the cabdriver and they got out of the cab. Kainan opened up the main door with his key and waved to the doorman. Reagan decided she would introduce herself later.

They rode the elevator, almost to the top, and down at the end of the hallway were two apartments. One was his and the other was hers.

She opened the door and saw the contents of her apartment were now in her new place. Her apartment on Richmond Street had been sparsely furnished, but because her old place had been smaller it had looked all right. Now she could see how sparse her belongings really were in this large new condo.

Kainan gestured and she followed him into a smaller room. He flicked on the lights and there was the crib, the chair and everything. All made up. Emotion overwhelmed her, and she covered her mouth to keep herself from crying.

It was too much. All of it. No one had ever shown her this kind of kindness or generosity before—not even her parents. Michael was like a father figure, but he had his own family. The only time she'd felt somewhat complete was when she was in Isla Hermosa with Kainan.

And then she'd thought he'd died.

Now this.

It was too much, and she wondered why she was fighting him. They could be a family.

She shook her head, because how *could* they be a family. How could she fall in love with a man who was King?

Are you okay? Kainan signed.

She nodded, overcome by his generosity. "It's wonderful. Thank you."

Kainan touched her face and then took her hand and placed it on his chest. Those dark eyes that had always been her downfall were tender and she couldn't help it.

She wanted to be with him.

Even if it was just one more time. She wanted to feel safe in his arms, to forget the world around them for just one moment. To forget all the horrors of this life and know that they had this. They shared so much.

She stepped closer and touched his face, running her fingers over the scars on his face and neck. He closed his eyes and under her other hand she could feel his heart beat faster. He wrapped his arms around her, pulling her against him.

Reagan closed her eyes and kissed him, melting into him as she had done so long ago. As she'd done a couple of days ago when he'd taken her to that room to calm down when she'd been so terrified of Peter having the surgery to attach the ventricular assist device.

Even without words he knew what she was

thinking. He knew what she needed. Who needed words when all that was needed was action? And in this moment, that was all she wanted.

She wanted to feel his arms around her again. Even if it was only one more time. She wanted him.

She didn't want to think. All she wanted to be was lost—in his arms, in his kisses. All she wanted to do was *feel*. She'd been numb for so long.

Kainan's kiss deepened and he pressed her against the door, their bodies flush together.

The kiss ended and those dark eyes glittered with desire.

"Yes," she whispered.

And that was all he needed.

He picked her up and carried her to the bedroom, where her bed was made up in the center of the very large room. There were no window coverings, and all she could see was the darkness of the lake outside her window. There were no other buildings, no one to look in and see them, just the darkness of the frigid water and the sound of another squall blowing in off the lake.

* * *

Kainan couldn't believe this was happening. It was what he wanted. All he'd ever wanted. There had been no other woman who'd made him feel this way.

He cupped her face as she undid his belt, watching her eyes, those beautiful brown eyes which made him weak in the knees, and those full pink lips he loved to kiss.

"All I want is you, Kainan. Right here. Right now."

And that was all he needed to hear. Like the snow squall that was raging outside the windows, there was a storm in his soul. He needed to possess her again and never let her go. There was no turning back for them.

Even though he wasn't supposed to use his voice, because of the scar tissue forming in his throat, he whispered against her lips. "No protection."

This seduction, making love to her, was a part of him that he'd thought long gone. He'd thought the Kainan he'd been before his brother had died and he'd became King was long gone. He'd been so focused on duty versus desire he had never

prepared for this moment when desire would win over. She made him forget his duty.

"It's okay," she said, kneeling in front of him and unbuttoning his shirt. "I'm on the pill. I won't get pregnant."

And what about last time? he signed, teasing her.

"I wasn't on the pill then. That was an entirely different situation."

He chuckled and leaned his head against hers. "You're…sure?"

"Yes. Very sure. I want you, Kainan."

She opened his shirt and ran her hands over his chest. Her simple touch made him burn with need for her. He wanted to possess her again and again. He'd lost all sense of reason.

There was no way he could turn back. She made him *feel*—made him feel as if he could breathe and love. Things that he'd thought he would never feel again.

And although he wasn't sure what was going to happen in his future, he knew one thing to be true—and that was he never wanted to let her go in this moment.

He kissed her again, running his hand down her

back, cupping her bottom to pull her tight against him. He didn't want any space between them and he didn't want to let her go.

All these thoughts ran through his mind. The things he wanted to tell her. How he'd thought only of her since they'd parted. How the memory of her had got him through so much.

How there was only her.

"I've missed you," she whispered, and then she let out a little moan of pleasure as he kissed her throat down to her collarbone, feeling her pulse quicken under his lips.

Kainan had nearly lost his mind with his want for her. *This* was what he'd been dreaming about for so long.

If he wasn't careful he would just take her— right here and now, half dressed—and he didn't want that. Not in this moment.

Kainan wanted to take his time with her.

He wanted to do right by her.

He'd been waiting so long for a chance. A chance to be with her again.

"Kainan…" she whispered, running her hands down his back, her touch leaving goose bumps across his skin.

He couldn't wait, and they made quick work of the rest of their clothes. He undid her rich mahogany brown hair from its confining bun and ran his fingers through the silken softness. Nothing was between them now. It was just the two of them… bared to each other and vulnerable.

I love your hands on my body, he thought as her hands moved over his skin.

"I can tell you like that," she whispered.

And then she continued teasing with her fingertips, running a finger down his neck, over his chest and lower. Her hand splayed against his abdomen before slipping lower and gripping his erection in the palm of her hand.

He groaned.

She chuckled, and then nibbled his neck. Every nerve-ending in his body was alive as she stroked him. His blood was on fire, and he tried to hold back another moan but couldn't keep it in. Reagan's touching him was driving him wild, and he was afraid that if she kept it up he would come. Only he didn't want her to stop.

Her mouth was on him now, and his hands slipped into her hair. His throat tightened but he

couldn't stop. The pleasure was making his body wild with need.

He pulled her away and pushed her against the mattress, pinning her there below him. Reagan bit her lower lip and tried to wrap herself around him, but he let go of her wrists to push open her legs.

"Kainan…" she begged.

He grinned, and wouldn't give in to her pleas.

"Kainan, what're you…? Oh, my God," she gasped as he did what she had done to him. Tortured her the way she had him, driving her wild with need.

"Please," she begged.

He didn't respond, just ran his tongue around the most sensitive part of her, making her cry out. He wanted her to come, but he wanted to be inside her too. He was greedy and he wanted all of her.

Reagan arched her hips up and he moved over her, staring down into her eyes, then bent down to kiss her as he entered her slowly.

He groaned. She was so tight, so hot. It took every ounce of his control not to take her fast. It had been so long since he'd been with her. There hadn't been another since her, he'd never had a desire for any other.

It was only her.

Just Reagan.

He sank deeper into her and quickened his pace. He couldn't hold back. He slipped a hand under her bottom, bringing her closer and angling his thrusts as he took all of her. It was hard to hold back, but he wanted Reagan to come first, and it didn't take long before she was crying out his name, tightening around him.

And that was when he sought his own release.

When it was over he rolled away, trying to catch his breath, but it was only a moment before he pulled her close against him. He didn't want her far from him. He needed her.

"Kainan…" she whispered in the darkness, her breath fast and heavy like his.

He ran his hands over her soft body and kissed her gently.

"Sleep," he said hoarsely. "I'm here."

Reagan smiled up at him and sighed.

Soon she was asleep, the even sound of her breathing letting him know she'd drifted off. The wind was howling outside, a high-pitched wail which usually set him on edge and made him

shiver, but there was no shivering with her warm body pressed against his.

Tonight he had her.

Tonight she was his Queen. Even if it was only for one night.

CHAPTER ELEVEN

THE ALARM WENT off at six o'clock in the morning. At first Kainan forgot for a moment why he'd set the alarm so early, because all he wanted to do was lie in Reagan's arms all day long. Then he remembered that it was Christmas Eve and Dr. Shaw wanted him at the hospital so he could do another MRI and check the extent of new damage and scar tissue in preparation for the surgery coming up soon.

Try as he might, Kainan hadn't been able to keep silent when he'd made love to Reagan. He'd lost all sense of logic and reason, and now he was paying for it.

His throat was hoarse, sore and very tight. It was hard to breathe, but last night had been worth it.

Kainan disentangled himself from Reagan's arms and slowly got out of bed.

"Where are you going?" she whispered, and

flicked on a light which blinded them both. "It's dark still."

I'm not trying to sneak away.

"Where are you off to then?" she asked, sitting up.

To the hospital.

"Is it Peter?" she asked, panicked.

No, it's me. He ran his hand through his hair. *I just need another MRI scan. There's more adhesions in my throat.*

"Oh," she said quietly, worried. "That will complicate the surgery."

Yes, and it also complicates my breathing, not just my voice.

She cocked an eyebrow. "I'm worried about you. Worried about this surgery."

He grinned and touched her face, whispering, "I am not."

It was a lie. He was, but there was no choice.

"What happens if you…? What happens to your country?"

Peter could be King.

Reagan frowned. "Peter is not legitimate."

You can change that.

She rolled her eyes and shook her head. "Are you crazy?"

Reagan, please. We belong together as a family.

She looked unsure, and for some reason he got an inkling that he was getting through to her. Maybe she would agree to be his Queen. Then he could take care of them.

That's if you survive the surgery.

He didn't want to think of that. He didn't want to think of putting Peter in a position of having no childhood. Perhaps he was being selfish, like his father. Still, he wanted both of them. He needed them both.

"I'm worried about this surgery, I really am," she said.

It touched him that she cared so much.

I don't know when or if I can have the surgery, he signed, and then started to pull on his discarded clothes.

"I'll go with you to the MRI."

He shook his head. *No, you need to go to Peter. They could be discharging him today. I will have a security detail available for you and a town car to bring you back here with him. Do you have a car seat?*

"I did…it's probably in the closet in his nursery."

He nodded. *I will be fine. I promise to keep you posted, and tonight we'll celebrate as a family.*

"Just don't do anything rash. You can be a voiceless king, Kainan. There is no shame in it."

I am not ashamed. I just want answers. If it can be resolved, then I would like to speak again—I would like to address my people. It was maddening not being able to work on my own during that trauma. I had to follow you like a shadow. I couldn't go into the operating room as lead surgeon because how can I sign with my hands inside a person? I have to return to my throne strong.

Kainan finished dressing.

Do not worry, Reagan. Everything will be okay. We'll order in food for tonight and celebrate our first Christmas, the three of us together.

She smiled. "You can invite Andreas and the other members of your security team. Andreas is family. He's Peter's uncle, whether he wants to admit it or not. And he cares for you."

I will try to convince him, but Andreas takes decorum very seriously. He didn't even want my blood. Kainan straightened his tie. *When the MRI is done I will come see you—or, if they decide*

to discharge Peter before I'm done, I will meet you here.

"Okay…" she said, but he could tell that there was uncertainty in her voice and he wished he could tell her more. Tell her how much he cared, but that he was scared. Scare of ruining it all. Scared of breaking her heart if he died.

The pressure he felt was keen.

As he left Reagan's apartment he ran into Andreas, who was limping to the apartment next door with a cane.

"Your Majesty," Andreas said, wincing as he tried to bow.

Don't. Kainan stopped him. *Rest. Diego, another one of my security guards, is taking me to the hospital for a test.*

"The MRI?" Andreas asked hopefully.

Yes.

Andreas looked worried. "I should be with you, Your Majesty."

It is fine. Reagan is next door. Keep an eye on her, if you must.

"You spent the night with her? Has she agreed to be Queen?"

Not yet. Rest, Andreas. That's an order.

"Thank you, Your Majesty."

Kainan nodded and went downstairs, where Diego was waiting for him. He didn't say much and opened the door to the tinted-windowed town car. Diego knew where Kainan needed to go.

First the MRI, then the embassy. Time was running out. Kainan had to put his affairs in order before he had surgery, and he was angry with himself for letting it go this long. But he'd been too afraid before.

Now, with Peter and Reagan, Kainan was experiencing something he had not felt in a long time, and that was hope. He was always going to make sure everyone was protected if he died on the operating table, but that hope gave him courage. He wasn't going to die during surgery. He was going to fight. He was going to live to know his son and to return to Isla Hermosa and take his place as King.

Reagan was torn.

Last night in Kainan's arms had been so amazing and it had felt right. She had felt as if she belonged with him. And then he'd shattered her by

telling her that he was still contemplating going through a risky procedure to restore his voice.

It wasn't so much the surgery itself that was terrible, but Kainan's injury...the scar tissue.

The idea was too much for her to bear, and she was torn between what she'd been taught her whole life and becoming a family with Kainan.

She found a towel in one of the boxes in her bedroom and had a quick shower in her brandnew walk-in shower.

When she walked out of the bathroom, she glanced out of the window toward the icy waters of Lake Ontario.

Right now it was full of foreboding. A stormy, gloomy body of water that had always freaked her out. But then she thought about the spring thaw and the summer, when she would be able to watch the ferry head from Queen's Quay to the islands, and that brought a smile to her face.

There was Centerville, out on one of those islands, and she thought about taking Peter there one day—taking all the rides with him and walking on the beaches there. She thought about all the things they could do. But now, instead of seeing only her and Peter in the picture, she saw Kainan.

Would it really be so bad to be his wife?

Once Peter had his new heart she could move to Isla Hermosa. Despite the war, she had enjoyed her time there—the ocean, the tropical weather and the lush jungle.

There was really nothing to keep her in Toronto after Peter got his heart. She could practice medicine in Isla Hermosa. Perhaps she could do even more, like teach the future physicians of Isla Hermosa. She'd always wanted to teach.

Maybe she *could* have it all?

Be careful. You can only rely on yourself.

She shook that thought away, because right now she was feeling something she had never felt before and that was love. The picture she had in her mind of her future didn't have to be Toronto or London, Ontario…it could be Isla Hermosa and Europe.

And Kainan.

She couldn't lose him again. She'd thought that she had lost him once and that had nearly destroyed her. This was her second chance, and she would be a fool not to take it, but she was terrified beyond all reason.

Reagan got dressed as quickly as she could and

then dug the car seat out of Peter's closet. Starting tonight, with Peter home for Christmas and Kainan here, she was going to make her life right.

She couldn't be scared anymore.

She wasn't going to ruin this second chance that she had been given.

As she locked her door, the door to Kainan's apartment opened and Andreas hobbled out.

"Andreas! They let you out?" she asked.

Andreas turned and smiled at her. "Yes, Dr. Cote. I am fine now."

"You need to rest," she said. "Where are you going?"

"Out. There is no food."

"You should order in."

Andreas sighed. "I was going to go to the hospital and check on Kainan."

"I thought someone else was with him? You really should rest."

"I should be the one to go to the hospital with him," Andreas said grimly.

"You really need to rest. But tonight come over and have dinner. You are family."

"I beg your pardon?" said Andreas.

"He told me that you're his illegitimate half brother."

Andreas frowned. "I wish he hadn't."

"Kainan cares about you."

Andreas sighed. "And I him."

"So come over and celebrate"

"No, it is not proper. There's nothing to celebrate. The surgery is too risky, and if he dies he will be leaving the country without an heir."

"It's a risky surgery, for sure, but—"

"The odds of his death are high."

Reagan's heart skipped a beat. "What are you talking about?"

"He has extensive scar tissue…"

"Kainan could *die*?" Her world spun out of control.

Andreas nodded. "Although your son could still be King if you marry him."

Reagan's heart sank. So that was why Kainan wanted to marry her. Why he constantly pestered her to marry him. It wasn't because he cared for her—it was all about the crown. It was all about saving his kingdom because he expected to die. He was going to abandon her and Peter after all, and abandon them to a life she didn't want.

If she hadn't had Peter then he probably wouldn't have bothered with her.

You've opened your heart to the wrong man, Reagan. You always do. This heartache is all your fault.

Reagan couldn't even respond to Andreas. She just turned on her heel and carried on her way. She didn't know what to think.

She was hurt that Kainan had used her. Played her for a fool. He didn't really care for her *or* Peter. He saw them as a means to save his country. To save its monarchy.

And it hurt.

Had their night of passion been a part of his game?

She slammed the "down" button at the elevator as hard as she could and it felt good to hit it—but it didn't quell the feelings of betrayal she was experiencing right now. The pain…

The fact he'd lied to her and hadn't even been able to tell her the truth.

Why had she thought she could trust him? She knew better than to listen to her heart. Her heart was thing that always got her into trouble. She was a fool.

She hailed a cab and climbed in, directing the taxi driver to take her to the hospital. She didn't know what she was going to do when she saw Kainan, but she knew one thing was for certain now. She was never going to marry.

Never.

CHAPTER TWELVE

AFTER KAINAN'S MRI he was scheduled for surgery with Dr. Shaw on December twenty-sixth in the morning. There were risks that the scar tissue was now threatening his ability to breathe, and that was not good. Dr. Shaw had put him on oxygen just now, and he was feeling light-headed because breathing was getting harder.

He had to get it done sooner rather than later.

When the surgery had bee booked he went straight to the embassy to talk to his delegates about his possible death.

Kainan had decided that it was time that the monarchy did not have absolute control over the people. Time for him to take a step back, so that if he died Peter would not be trapped as he had been.

He could be a figurehead, and he could help his people, but Kainan had to give them the tools to help themselves, and soon his delegates would be

in the process of dealing with the Canadian officials in order to make that happen.

Which meant the deadline for him to be crowned was a moot point. He had it struck out in one of his last acts of power.

The burden that had been lifted from his shoulders was great.

He felt free.

He was still King, but it was different.

This was now a monarchy on his own terms—a monarchy that would serve its people. They could vote in a prime minister. There would be a democracy.

And Kainan would oversee these things to make sure corrupt people didn't get into power as long as he was their figurehead.

When he got to the hospital he went straight to Peter's room to talk to Reagan, but when he got there the room was empty.

Peter was gone and so was Reagan.

His heart lurched and he began to panic, thinking that something had happened to their son.

A pediatric nurse came into the room. "Dr. Laskaris, they've been discharged. They were dis-

charged about twenty minutes ago, so they're probably at home."

Kainan breathed a sigh of relief and mouthed his thanks to the nurse before rushing out of the hospital. He was texting Diego when he saw Andreas limping in.

Dammit.

"Your Majesty," Andreas said. He looked concerned.

What's wrong? Kainan asked.

"It's Dr. Cote. She knows. She knows about the risks of your surgery."

His stomach sank like a rock. *How does she know? Did the press find out?*

Andreas shook his head. "I told her."

Kainan saw red, felt his blood boiling, and it took every ounce of his strength not to hit Andreas.

You did what?

"Your Majesty, I had to tell her. I am also the one who broke into her apartment."

Why would you do that?

"I wanted to push her into your arms. I wanted to protect my country and your birthright. Your son's birthright."

Kainan mouthed a few choice curse words and scrubbed a hand over his face. *I can't believe you did this, Andreas. You've ruined everything!*

"How? She knows the truth now."

I was going to tell her, but I was also going to tell her that the monarchy no longer exists.

Andreas was confused. "I don't understand…"

I'm forming a democracy, Andreas. I will still be King, but I will just be a figurehead. I will help the people rebuild Isla Hermosa and they will vote in a prime minster and elect officials. The people will run Isla Hermosa. I will not.

Andreas blinked and then bowed his head, ashamed. "Your Majesty, I'm sorry that I doubted your abilities."

Kainan sighed and gripped his half brother's shoulders. *It's all right. I just pray that it's not too late to turn this around with Reagan. I still want her as my Queen, but only when she wants to become my Queen. And Peter can inherit one day, but he doesn't have to. There will be a government.*

"I'm glad to hear that, Your Majesty."

Andreas turned and they walked out of the hospital together.

Have the police come for you yet? Kainan asked.

"No, I know how to get away with murder, Your Majesty," Andreas teased. "I can fake an apartment break-in without being caught."

Kainan smiled. *I will still need a head of security, but I think that you should run for prime minister when we go back to Isla Hermosa. You would be a fine elected leader. You're a war hero, as was your father before you.*

Andreas nodded. "Perhaps—but right now I want to make sure you and your family are taken care of."

Kainan hugged Andreas. *I'm still ticked off at you for sticking your nose in where it doesn't belong.*

"I know, but if I hadn't then everything would've been lost."

Diego pulled up in front of the hospital and Kainan helped Andreas in first and then climbed in himself. He had to make things right with Reagan before it was too late.

When they got to the apartment Diego helped Andreas out and Kainan ran inside. At least he knew that she would be there. Everything of hers

was still there, and he had a key so she couldn't lock him out.

When he got to their floor he passed a locksmith and saw Reagan standing in the doorway, her arms crossed and her face like thunder.

He started to sign. *Let me explain—*

"Save it," she said. "Andreas told me everything."

Not everything.

"He told me that you needed me to marry you so you can legitimize Peter and that when you die he'll be King? Is that correct, or is there more to that story?" she asked.

That was true, but now there is more.

She raised an eyebrow. "I'm listening."

That was true up until this afternoon. Now I have changed everything. I don't need to marry you for Peter to be King.

Reagan reeled as if she had been slapped. "How nice for you."

Reagan, I'm creating a democracy. I will just be a figurehead now.

She didn't say anything, but he saw he was getting through to her. She hadn't shut him out yet.

Peter will become King whether we are married

or not, he signed. *And he too will only be a fig-
urehead. Isla Hermosa is to become a democracy.
And with that the old monarchy was replaced.
My officials at the embassy and back home are
working with the prime ministers of Canada and
Britain to make this happen. There will be peace
now because of this.*

"I'm very happy to hear there will be peace,"
she said softly.

But...?

"You lied to me. You constantly asked me to
marry you because you said you wanted to pro-
tect me."

I did.

"You *did*?" she asked, her eyes shining with
tears. "And that's the trouble. Now that I'm not
needed anymore, you're free. You don't need me."

Reagan, I still want to protect you.

"I wish I could believe that, Kainan. I really
wish I could. But first you lie to me and then
you don't tell me that you're King of a country.
You don't contact me and tell me that you're still
alive."

*I couldn't tell you I was alive. I was in hiding.
Besides, I didn't know where in Canada you were.*

Reagan ignored him. "You told me your surgery was risky, but not how risky. Why did you feel the need to lie to me?"

To protect you!

She nodded. "I don't believe it. I can't. You've broken my trust, Kainan. You've hurt me too much. You're welcome to be a part of Peter's life, but I will fight you if you try and take him out of Canada and away from me. He's too fragile to live a life like yours."

Reagan, please don't turn me away.

Although he wouldn't blame her for doing so. And he couldn't sign the words he needed to say because he wanted to *say* them. To use his own words to tell her he loved her.

I need you, Reagan. I want you in my life.

Reagan sighed and a tear slipped down her cheek. "I wish I could believe that, Kainan. I wish that I could."

She turned back into her apartment and shut the door. Shutting him out of her life.

He sighed sadly, but he wasn't giving up.

He'd come too far to give up on her now.

Even if she didn't want to marry him, he was

going to have Reagan in his life and he would do anything to win her back.

He would not be the man his father had been.

It was heartbreaking to spend Peter's first Christmas alone with him, especially when she'd thought Kainan would be there.

She'd thought for a brief moment that they were becoming a family—and then she'd found out the real reason why he wanted a family.

To protect the crown when he died.

He needed them, but not in the way she'd hoped he would. Did he even really *want* them?

Still, this was the way she'd *thought* she was going to spend Peter's first Christmas, when she'd been pregnant with him and had thought Kainan was dead.

It was scary how dependent she'd become on Kainan without really realizing. She'd got used to having him around.

They had even planned to spend Peter's first Christmas together, but since she'd turned him away on Christmas Eve she hadn't seen him.

It was now Boxing Day, and she was considering going next door and talking to him. Perhaps

she'd been too harsh on him. She wanted him involved in Peter's life, but that was it. They could work together for as long as he was at the hospital, and they could work together to raise Peter, but that was where she had to draw the line.

She couldn't risk her heart again.

But you love him. Love is always worth the risk.

Her phone started ringing and she answered it.

"Reagan, it's Michael."

He sounded completely stressed out.

"Michael? Is everything okay?"

"UNOS called. There's a match, and I've sent a recovery team to Ottawa to get it. There's a heart for your son. You need to bring Peter in right away."

Her heart skipped a beat.

So soon.

She'd only just got him home. She had been enjoying her time with him and now she had to take him back and put him in the hands of the surgeons.

"I'll be right there. Thank you, Michael."

Reagan hung up the phone. She could hear Peter stirring through the baby monitor.

She grabbed the baby monitor and left her apart-

ment, heading straight to Kainan's. She knocked on the door. She could feel panic rising.

Diego answered the door. "Dr. Cote?"

"Is Kainan here?"

"No," Diego said. "Andreas took His Majesty over to the hospital early this morning to have his surgery."

"His surgery? Right…that's today too."

The world began to spin out of control. Peter and Kainan were both having surgery on the same day. She could potentially lose them both.

"Is everything okay, Dr. Cote?"

"Can I get a ride to the hospital? It's Peter—they've found him a heart."

"Yes, of course. I will meet you downstairs in ten minutes."

Reagan nodded and went back to her apartment as Diego closed the door. She went straight to Peter, who smiled when she entered the room.

Her body shook and she smiled back at him. "My little love," she whispered as she carefully picked him up and held him tight.

What if this was the last time she got to hold him? What if he didn't survive?

Right now she wasn't in the mind-set of a sur-

geon. She was in the mind-set of a mother who was terrified about what she might lose.

And Kainan was going to have surgery too.

She could lose it all in one fell swoop.

She had to make things right.

Reagan kissed Peter's head. "I'm going to make it right for you. I swear."

She would do better for her son than her parents ever had for her.

She packed up Peter's ventricular device and got him into his car seat, covering him with a blanket. She grabbed everything Peter needed and hurried out of the apartment.

Kainan was in pre-op with Andreas. He wanted to see Reagan. He'd gotten word that a heart for Peter had been found.

Screw this.

He got out of the bed where he'd been waiting for Dr. Shaw.

"Your Majesty?" Andreas said in alarm.

Tell Dr. Shaw I will be back in time for my surgery. I have to see Reagan and Peter.

Andreas nodded. "Yes, Your Majesty."

Kainan pulled on his street clothes and left the

room. His throat was tight and his pulse was racing. He cleared his throat and rolled his shoulders. It was hard to breathe. It had been getting harder to breathe since Reagan had locked him out of her life.

She was his air. His freedom. And he needed her.

It was stress that was making him feel this way, and he knew he wouldn't relax until he saw Peter and Reagan.

He made his way to the pediatric floor, where they were prepping Peter. He could hear him crying. He'd never heard him cry before. Reagan hadn't let him see him since he'd been discharged two days ago. Not that he blamed her. He'd ruined everything by not telling her the truth.

Hearing Peter cry was an amazing thing.

It was strong.

Reagan turned around and her expression softened, making his heart skip a beat. He wanted to comfort her, but didn't want her to push him away.

"What're you doing here?" Reagan asked.

I'm his father, Kainan signed.

"I know, but I thought you would be in pre-op yourself."

Who told you?

"Diego. You're going through with it?"

Of course.

"You could die," she said, biting her lip as if she was holding something back. "If you're just to be a figurehead then you don't need to go through with this surgery. There are less riskier surgeries to remove adhesions."

I do.

"Kainan, it's too risky."

He nodded. *So is this.*

They both turned to Peter as the gurney came in and the pediatric cardiologist, Dr. Bruni, entered the room.

"Reagan and Kainan." He nodded at them both. "The heart is on its way from the airport. We're now going to take Peter into surgery and remove the ventricular device and put him on bypass. You both know the procedure. He will be in the pediatric critical care unit for some time and will be on anti-rejection drugs for the rest of his life."

Reagan nodded and Kainan felt numb.

She stepped forward and kissed Peter goodbye.

Kainan took a step toward his son. The last time he'd gone off to surgery Kainan hadn't even been

able to look at him. It had been too painful—as was this.

What if something happened and he didn't ever get to know his son?

What if he died in the operating room himself?

Better me than Peter.

He touched his son's head and then kissed him. He couldn't say that he loved him. He had no voice with which to say it. But he hoped Peter knew that he did.

He couldn't lose Peter. Kainan wanted time with him. Parents were never supposed to outlast their own children, though he'd seen it every day when he was a surgeon.

Life was complicated and messy. And he wanted Peter to experience it all.

He stepped back and they wheeled Peter away.

Reagan broke down in tears, sobbing into her hands, her shoulders shaking. Kainan took her in his arms and she clung to him.

"I'm sorry," she whispered against his neck. "I'm so sorry."

When she looked up he signed, *What for?*

"For pushing you away. I never gave you a chance to explain anything. You were carrying around this tremendous burden and I should've

been more sympathetic. I know what it's like to carry around a burden as big as that, and I'm sorry I didn't give you the chance. I was afraid."

Of what?

"Of relying on you and losing you. I've never had anyone before. Never had love…or a family. Not really."

Me neither.

"Only you have ever cared for me."

I understand. I had people to rely on, people to protect me, and I was never alone—but I really was. I was scared of relying on you too, Reagan. I was scared of...

Kainan felt his throat tighten and he touched her face. The room began to spin and he shook his head, trying to focus.

He was finding it hard to breathe.

And he couldn't call for help.

He couldn't tell her what was happening.

"Kainan?" she said, panic in her voice.

I love you. That was the last thought he had before everything went black.

Reagan screamed out as Kainan's knees buckled under him and she helped him to the floor. As she

laid him out she couldn't hear any breath sounds. She hit the panic button on the wall to call a code and then she tried to breathe for him, compressing his chest to keep his heart beating.

He'd stopped breathing.

She couldn't lose him for real this time.

She hadn't even had a chance to tell him that she loved him. That she forgave him and that she wanted to try and make it work. That she was tired of carrying her burden alone and that she now knew it was okay not to handle everything on your own.

It was okay to lean on someone else—especially someone you loved.

The code team came for him. They got a tube down his throat and started manually ventilating him.

She had to take a step back.

She couldn't work on him.

They whisked him off to surgery.

"I can't lose him," Reagan said out loud to herself. "I thought I'd lost him once. I can't go through that again."

And she made a vow then and there that if Kai-

nan came out of surgery she was going to make things right—just as she'd promised Peter.

She needed Kainan. She loved him.

As much as she had been taught that she didn't need anyone, she knew she needed Kainan and he needed her. She wasn't going to squander her second chance.

Not this time.

Pain was the first thing that Kainan felt. His throat was raw, as if it had been shredded with a thousand razor blades. His mouth was dry.

It took him a moment to realize what was happening and then he remembered. He had been with Reagan and they had just taken Peter away when he'd collapsed.

He tried to sit up, but it hurt.

"Don't try and sit up," Reagan said gently.

Kainan opened his eyes and smiled at her. He signed to ask her what had happened.

"Scar tissue blocked your airway. Dr. Shaw was able to get at it all, and repair your vocal cords, though it may be a few days before you will be able to speak. If you can't speak don't worry—it will come. You're in the ICU, still."

Peter? he asked, signing.

Reagan grinned, her smile bright. "He made it through. He did beautifully and is in the pediatric critical care unit."

Kainan let out a sigh of relief. *I want to go see him.*

"We will. You're still coming out of the sedation. Dr. Shaw wanted to make sure that you had some extra rest after your surgery yesterday, so he kept you in a medicated coma for a night."

What day is it?

"The twenty-ninth. The New Year is coming and your move to a democracy went through. Your coronation will wait and your people are voting for their first prime minister."

I am sorry about all that.

Reagan touched his face. "I know, and I'm sorry that I didn't give you a proper chance. I was so scared of relying on anyone. I've been used to doing things on my own for so long."

You have no reason to apologize.

"I do. I was devastated when I thought you were dead, Kainan. It crushed me. It felt like I'd lost my best friend, my partner, and then you came back and you were so distant. It killed me. I just didn't

want to risk my heart. I wasn't even sure that I was feeling anything, what with Peter."

I am the one who needs to apologize. I left you alone and I didn't try and reach out to you. You carried our son alone, dealt with his devastating diagnosis alone. I should've been there. I felt like I was failing you the way I failed my brother.

"You didn't fail your brother—he failed you *and* your country," she said.

He shook his head. *I should have tried harder to stop him. I could've done more to control him. And then maybe, just maybe, there wouldn't have been a war. Lives could've been spared.*

"Everything happens for a reason, Kainan. You weren't your brother's keeper. You did the best you could."

I'm sorry, Reagan. I'm sorry for deceiving you, for abandoning you. I love you more than anything.

Reagan leaned over and kissed him. "I love you too. And, if the offer still stands, I would like to be your wife."

Kainan grinned. *It will always stand, but are you sure? I have to return to Isla Hermosa at some point. Your home is here in Toronto.*

"My home is with you and our son. That's all the home I need." They kissed again. "I love you so much, Kainan."

"I love you too," he whispered.

Kainan developed a slight postoperative fever, which was not uncommon after the amount of blood that he'd lost. So he wasn't allowed to see Peter until New Year's Eve.

As he walked to the pediatric critical care unit, with Andreas following closely behind with a wheelchair, he couldn't help but think about how this should have been the night he'd prepared for this coronation. Now, instead of a coronation, a parliament was being formed. It was an exciting time for Isla Hermosa and he couldn't wait to go back.

As soon as Kainan and Peter had healed, they would go back to Isla Hermosa and begin to heal the country—from the ground up.

Kainan had decided that the palace would be repaired, but would no longer be his home. It would instead house the new government that was being formed right now.

He much preferred his original home outside the

city gates of Helicia—if it still stood. From there he could see the ocean and the beach. It reminded him of his mother and her longing to be free.

And, though he was still King, he would have more freedom now that Isla Hermosa was a democracy.

He wanted a safe place for Peter to play—not a prison for him to grow up in, like Kainan had had.

Reagan had been by his side. She'd moved between the rooms, taking care of him *and* Peter. Now that they were getting closer to the pediatric critical care unit, where Peter was, Kainan became nervous. Peter was no longer sedated and Kainan had never yet got to look into his eyes. Not really.

They put on gowns and were buzzed in.

Kainan walked toward his son's crib.

Peter was cooing and kicking, despite the incision in his chest.

As soon as Reagan came into view Peter responded happily to her presence and Kainan's heart melted.

He moved closer to the crib and Peter's eyes locked on his. Peter stared at him and Kainan could see eyes so similar to his studying him.

Emotion overcame him as he reached out and touched his son. Peter grasped his finger, squeezing it before smiling up at him.

Kainan's heart swelled, and instead of signing he opened his mouth, to hear his voice—not a whisper, but his *voice*—respond to his son.

"I love you."

He was no longer voiceless. He had a voice, his son had a new heart, and the three of them together were one. They were whole and healed.

EPILOGUE

Two years later, New Year's Eve, Isla Hermosa

"IT'S ALMOST TIME, Your Majesties," Andreas said, bowing as he came into the room.

Kainan's pulse was racing as he smoothed his hand over the traditional red military dress jacket that had once been worn by his father. His pulse was racing.

"You can do this."

Kainan smiled down at Reagan, who was dressed in white and wearing his mother's tiara, as well as some other jewels that had been hidden and saved during the war.

He sighed and nodded.

This was to be his first speech in Isla Hermosa since he'd returned, married Reagan and introduced the world to his son Peter, who was taking to his new heart so well. He'd spoken to his people briefly, but hadn't given his first address

in the new parliament that had been built in the restored palace.

Which was where he was now standing.

He was dressing in his mother's old room.

He, Reagan and Peter lived in his mother's seaside villa, outside the capital city of Helicia.

For the first year after his return Kainan had kept to himself as he and Peter had healed.

His surgery had been a success, but it had taken some time for him to speak properly again. There were times he was still unsure of his voice.

Reagan took his hand and squeezed it. "Your voice is strong. You can do this."

"Did I tell you…?" He took a pause. "How beautiful you look?"

She blushed. "Don't even *try* to get out of this by complimenting me. I'm not letting you off the hook."

Kainan chuckled and held out his arm. "Are you ready for this moment? Standing by my side as I address parliament?"

"No!" She laughed nervously as she slipped her arm over his. "I'm afraid I'm going to mess something up. I'd rather be at the free clinic in town."

Kainan beamed at her. "You're giving my se-

curity team a hard time, you know. Andreas is finding it difficult to calm Diego down when you work at the clinic."

"Why?" she asked. "It's perfectly safe. I'm a *surgeon*, Kainan. You promised me I could continue as a surgeon. I don't want the crown jewels or the palace. I just want to work."

"You just want to work?" he teased. "What about the beach house and our son?"

"Well, of course. And there's also one more thing," Reagan said.

"What's that?"

"You."

She kissed him—just a light feather kiss, but it made his blood fire and he suddenly didn't want to be there any longer.

"Diego is very concerned about you working in the clinic."

"Why?" she asked.

"Diego can't stand the sight of blood."

"He should leave the room, then."

Kainan shook his head. "He's devoted to his Queen. He cannot."

Reagan's arm trembled. "I'm not used to that."

"You're doing fine."

Then Andreas opened the door.

Kainan held Peter's hand. Peter laughed and smiled at his parents. And Kainan's tension melted away.

In his son he saw himself, but he also saw Reagan. Peter had Reagan's spirit—the spirit that reminded him of his mother.

Every day Peter grew stronger, and their life in Isla Hermosa grew more idyllic. The beach house was the perfect hideaway for them to live in peace.

"Your Majesty," Andreas said with a hint of pride. "Prime Minister Monterro is ready for you."

"I am ready," Kainan said, but inside he was nervous.

This was the first time he would be addressing his people since the successful election of Alejandro Monterro as their first prime minster. Judging by the way Isla Hermosa had bloomed in the last couple of years, Alejandro was the perfect choice. And Kainan respected him.

Reagan squeezed his arm.

As Kainan escorted Reagan through the door he reached down with the hand that had been rest-

ing on his ceremonial sword and took his son's chubby hand in his.

"You're breaking protocol," Reagan whispered.

"I think that it does not matter anymore," Kainan whispered back.

They smiled at each other.

The three of them walked side by side towards the double doors. One the other side was Isla Hermosa's parliament and a handful of reporters. Not only were his people watching, the whole world was watching.

Before the double doors opened Kainan turned to Reagan and she let go his hand and took Peter, because he had to walk in alone first.

"I couldn't have done this without you," he said, touching her cheek.

"You were always going to have the surgery—your voice would've been restored."

"I know, but you're the reason I'm alive. You and Peter have given me a reason to live. I love you."

Reagan's eyes glistened with tears. "And I love you."

"Me too," Peter chirped.

Kainan laughed and tousled his son's hair. He turned to Andreas and nodded. "I'm ready now."

Andreas beamed and opened the doors.

Kainan was blinded by bright lights, flashing bulbs.

"His Majesty, King Kainan the First!"

It was shouted over the din of scraping chairs as everyone stood.

Kainan gripped the hilt of his sword tightly, taking a step through the double doors into what had once been his father's throne room, but now held Isla Hermosa's democracy—

It was a step towards his destiny.

A destiny not only as a king, but as a father and husband.

As a man who had once again found his voice. A voice he never would have found if it hadn't been for Reagan.

This was all for her and Peter.

There was no turning back—and, thanks to Reagan, he never wanted to.

With her by his side he could do anything.

* * * * *